Sit-Down Money

KAY CHAPMAN

BALBOA.
PRESS

A DIVISION OF HAY HOUSE

Balboa Press books may be ordered through booksellers or by contacting:

Balboa Press
A Division of Hay House
1663 Liberty Drive
Bloomington, IN 47403
www.balboapress.com.au
1 (877) 407-4847

Cover imagery and graphics by Brooke McDonald Design, Brisbane, Australia
© 2017 Kay Chapman

Print information available on the last page.

ISBN: 978-1-5043-0668-3 (sc)
ISBN: 978-1-5043-0669-0 (e)

Balboa Press rev. date: 03/13/2017

Acknowledgements

The author acknowledges, with gratitude and deepest respect, Australia's First People. Their ability to endure many challenges, both prior to and following invasion by other races, is deeply revered. As a people they have overcome adversity.

I also acknowledge the many health staff whose work within the rural and remote communities of Australia has contributed to understanding and mutual learning.

I am thankful to my husband and my wonderful family and friends who have urged the birth of this book following a very long gestation.

One of my family: My brother-in-law, Kevin Rogers, deserves special mention. He passed away on 5 April 2012. I dedicate *Sit-Down Money* to him, for without his critique and encouragement, this story may never have progressed past conceptualisation.

Kay Chapman

Chapter One

Arnhem Land, Australia-1987

Gina struggled to unfold her cramped legs, grateful she had worked hard, over her adult lifetime, to retain her agility. Her average height rarely inhibited her professional success, and in the past she had been pleased not to tower over her taller contemporaries.

She ducked through the doorway like a giraffe exiting a shoebox and stumbled down the narrow steps as they unfolded in front of her onto the red earthen runway. She clutched her last symbol of a past life: a favourite lamp that she had protectively nursed all the way from Melbourne to Nhulunbuy and Nhulunbuy to Lumbarta Island. A wall of searing heat engulfed her as she furtively adjusted her sunglasses to screen the bright sunlight. The heat was like none she had ever experienced, and she was sure she was slowly melting. The six-seater plane had been claustrophobic, but at least the airflow had kept the temperature to an endurable level. The intensity of the hot air singed her nasal passages and hampered her chest expansion as she tried to catch her breath.

Fine red dust promptly embedded in her pores as perspiration trickled between her breasts and down the small of her back, adhering her perfectly laundered white blouse to her skin, like a soaked shower curtain. The hot, light breeze brought the smell of saltbush, fired by occasional bursts of acrid aviation fuel. Gina Atkins wondered why this had been her dream.

A tired, rusting tin shed stood alone amid the saltbush at the edge of the unsealed airstrip. Fuel drums were scattered around it in a haphazard manner. Her concern accelerated as she noticed that the only other things that moved were the crests of the saltbush, rustled by the gentle hot breeze, and a distant, rising cloud of red dust.

Gina's mind raced back to her departure from the cool comfort she had enjoyed at Melbourne's Qantas club lounge, the ice tingling in her gin and tonic. What on earth had she been thinking? How could she have believed this wilderness was where she was destined to be? Compounding her alienation was the knowledge that she was now committed to living in a 'no alcohol' community.

Pilot Marc who delivered Gina to Lambarta Island, was bemused by her obvious anxiety. Preparing to depart he climbed to the top of the aircraft stairs and stopped and turned. "Well, Gina, good luck— you'll need it!" he said teasingly. "I gotta go—due back in Nhulunbuy by five. See ya!" Even in her moment of desertion, she couldn't help noticing the cheeky allure of this young man and his very sexy arse. She silently reprimanded herself for allowing Alexa's frivolous words to pierce her consciousness: "a quick fuck from a young buck." *My, it has been a long time*, she thought, justifying herself.

Marc again hesitated. "Don't worry, Gina. You'll be fine. Just give it some time. Look after that lamp." Adding, "Hope the power is on tonight" chuckled Marc. Gina was unsure of the seriousness of his comment and looked to him for reassurance. None came. He waved goodbye and closed the aircraft door behind him. The engine sprang to life on command, and the aircraft turned and headed for the end of the dirt airstrip in preparation for take-off. On board too, was Gina's resolve.

Gina felt so very alone and desolate. She wanted to call after the pilot, "Don't leave me, Marc—I've made a terrible mistake! Take me back with you!" Her anxiety rose to greater heights as she steeled herself, trying to muster a little of the courage and conviction that had forsaken her.

She remembered well the night she had come to the decision to uproot her life and follow this insanity, and the many hours of hard work and effort it had taken to get here. She had revived her childhood longing. She had relived, time and again, the vulnerability and sadness she had suffered during her previous encounters with remote Australia.

Standing on the patio of one of Melbourne's most fashionable apartments, overlooking the city's horizon and the busy streetscape with its myriad of lights and sounds, Gina was struck by the beauty of the moon. It took her beyond earthly mayhem to the heights of celestial dreams. It seemed to seduce the foreboding clouds of the winter sky, its silver aura outlining the heavy grey masses as they moved across the sky. The smell of rain was in the air, mingling with the odours of the city and its wet bitumen. She revelled in the cool, crisp air that aided her solitude, heralding purity and serenity in contrast the cacophony of traffic, laughter, voices, and loud music. Gina struggled with her deepening unrest.

This post-awards party was not unlike many she had previously attended. As a successful fledgling model, she had looked to such occasions with excitement and anticipation. In the recent past, she had attended out of a sense of duty and expectation. She knew she scrubbed up OK for a forty-five-year-old who had weathered the challenges and temptations of the fashion world. Five years previously she had taken on a high-pressure desk job, with its overindulgent lunches and long hours of work, and managed to maintain a figure envied by women and admired by men. Honey-blonde wisps of hair gently caressed her handsome face and the nape of her neck, which was exposed by the artful way she swirled her hair into a twist and secured it to her head. Regular exercise and an abundant dose of good genes had helped her retain her slim figure and unblemished fair complexion.

Gina enjoyed a natural sense of chic that permeated her appearance and gestures. It was a quality that had been kind to her as she navigated her career from fashion model to fashion editor. She had unashamedly and gratefully used it to advantage in both her personal and professional life. Her coiffure and elegance had played a part in her persuasion of the impressionable but lecherous state minister, Albert Swanson, to look favourably upon an application for grant funding for a women's shelter. Her role on the board of the shelter, fundraising, was complete. She felt no guilt or remorse in using her womanly attributes to benefit other women, and would miss her volunteer work and the many friends she had made.

What was it that remained elusive? What niggled at her sense of fulfilment? Gina was aware that many saw her life as complete, enviable. They thought she had "done it all," and it concerned her that something within her continued to gnaw. Surrounded by people she loved and whose company she enjoyed, Gina felt alone. She found it hard to explain, because her feelings were elusive and beyond forming into words.

Her divorce from Aiden had been finalised two years previously. Her life with her daughter, Savannah, was predictable but fun. Gina had watched Savannah's journey from girl to beautiful young woman with great pride and pleasure. Now eleven, Savannah had a good sense of self and a streak of determination that Gina was sure must have come from her father. They shared an attractive apartment close to the private ladies' college Savannah attended. Life was indeed comfortable.

Gina's river of reflection again drifted to the night sky. What of the life it blanketed beyond the city? Where were the stars tonight? Her musing took her back to the dreams and experiences of her girlhood and the innate knowledge that her fate was preordained. She examined her feelings of disappointment and realised that dreams were yet to be fulfilled. Did this hold the key to her despondency? Many would assume that her achievements had far exceeded those girlish whims. What more could one ask for than acclaim, wealth, and a position as fashion editor for *Women's Love* magazine?

"Gina, there you are. I've been searching all over this goddamned, smoke-ravaged, alcoholic orgy for you. What the fuck are you doing out here in the freezing cold?"

On hearing the raucous voice of her friend Alexa, Gina's thoughts snapped back to the party and the present.

Gina turned to her friend and smiled. "Alexa, it's a pleasure to see you too—just the tonic I need. As always, you exaggerate somewhat. I was merely enjoying a 'meaning of life' moment. But if it had to be disturbed by anyone, I'm glad it was you. You always bring me clarity laced with challenge. How are you, and what mischief have you been up to since I saw you last?" Gina's way of speaking was the antithesis of Alexa's: soothing, well enunciated, and polished.

Alexa Smyth-Parker was a rough diamond and one of the few in the fashion industry whom Gina not only admired but considered to be a true friend. Many people purporting to be friends were in fact industry whores— ready and willing to change allegiances, available only when they benefited and interested in no one other than themselves.

Alexa plonked her rotund bottom on the patio chair, proclaiming it "cold enough to freeze the balls off a brass monkey." Her ample legs spread out in her usual non-poised posture as she slumped into position. She was younger than Gina in years. Her mannerisms portrayed a frivolous woman. Gina knew better. She had seen many come off the poorer due to Alexa's vitriolic tongue when they made this wrong assumption. Gina also admired the deep respect with which Alexa was held throughout the industry.

Her persona fitted well with her flaming red, short-cropped hair. She was not a beautiful woman, but her vivacious, outgoing personality ensured that she was noticed. Provided her language could be overlooked, she could hold any audience with her colourful vocabulary, humour, and portrayal of life events.

Alexa was a professional competitor of Gina's. She held the position of manager on a rival magazine, *Femme Fatale*. While they had rarely shared emerging information, they spent many hours reflecting on the industry and deconstructing published articles— their own and those of others in the landscape. Gina enjoyed their frequent lunchtime meetings and had derived some great ideas from Alexa, as Alexa had from her. Gina valued Alexa's critique of her work. Alexa was a straight shooter and an astute businesswoman, and Gina was always confident of an honest opinion from her. Alexa was intolerant of fools but tremendously supportive of a chosen few. Beneath her brazen facade she was kind and caring. She was quick witted but never backbiting. You knew exactly where you stood with Alexa because she had no hesitation in telling you. They shared a deep mutual respect. Most of all, Alexa could nearly always read Gina like a book.

Alexa launched into a succession of tales about her recent sexual conquests and business dealings. She was an animated storyteller, and Gina soon became engrossed in her conversation. They negotiated their way back indoors mingling with other partygoers. Alexa was busy enumerating the superior qualities of her latest lover as they each collected a glass of champagne from a passing waiter.

Alexa's eyes followed the waiter. "Umm … Nice arse. I do like a bit of young stuff occasionally. A good fuck from a young buck keeps the hormones flowing and the body going, my love." She nudged Gina and winked conspiratorially.

Gina was caught off guard. She wondered how Alexa's simplification of life and statement of fact could still surprise her after their years of friendship. Gina laughed. "You're incorrigible. But I love you. I should probably warn that poor lad about women like you, but then it's nice to see the shoe on the other foot these days—old tarts after young bucks instead of old farts after young fillies."

Their laughter was concluded by a quick hug.

Gina's feelings again began to overwhelm her. She felt she could no longer keep up a pretence of enjoyment and interest in the fickle activities of her associates. Gina stopped. She felt emotionally drained, her laughing words ceasing a little too abruptly and her head bowing slightly to hide the betrayal of her feelings by her expressive face.

"Gina, what is it? What's up with you lately? Not getting enough, eh? I can easily fix that."

Alexa had known her for too long to have missed the edge to her present demeanour. Before Gina could begin to try to explain that which she didn't understand herself, they were joined by Rory de Flon, a robust Canadian radio announcer who worked at Radio 3GX. Rory liked to groove with the "in" set. He thrust himself upon them, encircling them in his large embrace. He then proceeded to make lewd comments about Alexa's sex life and her business balls.

Alexa was more than capable of giving as well as she got, and launched into a scathing attack on his rapidly developing paunch. "It's a good thing your adoring fans have fallen in love with your voice and not your body." She slapped his protruding tummy. "Is this the Aussie souvenir you're planning on taking home at Christmas, eh? You know, you should be very proud of your true blue, beer-swollen gut. Now you not only speak Aussie, you look like the real thing. But tell me, Rory, I've always wondered—how on earth do you accurately point percy to the porcelain these days? It must be hard to find such a tiny thing under those rolls."

Rory exploded into laughter and responded in a deep, uncharacteristically quiet voice, "Lower, baby, lower—then it will be plenty big enough to find."

This brought a look of pretend disdain from Gina and a chuckle from Alexa. Gina had long ago come to accept Alexa's candour and guile, as these were the qualities that Gina found most endearing about her friend. They admired and respected each other's intelligence and individuality. Gina's decorum never failed her. While Alexa often dug them into an uncomfortable situation, Gina always managed to use her sense of propriety and compassion to extricate them.

Gina's strong sense of self had grown out of her success. She took life more seriously. Despite her harsh upbringing of religious contrition and control, she had developed a dry sense of humour and deep compassion for those less fortunate. Alexa was one of a few people with whom Gina felt able to share her story of discovery. She had been extremely excited by the opportunities on offer beyond their meagre outback home. The elation was not shared by her disapproving mother.

Gina had been born to God-fearing country folk. She felt she was loved but never shown affection. The eldest of seven children, she bore unfettered responsibility for her siblings. By the age of thirteen, she had become their main carer. Her mother, Audrey, toiled alongside her father on the farm and supported him in his ministrations to the sinners of the outback. Household duties were Gina's responsibility. For the development of her planning and organisational skills, Gina was grateful to her mother. For her dry Irish humour, she was indebted to her father. For the loss of her childhood, she was regretful and envious of her peers. For the little time her father got to spend with his family prior to his premature death, she felt cheated.

Her father, James, had been ordained at the age of thirty-two and had taken up a posting in a remote area that bordered three states: New South Wales, Northern Territory, and Queensland-Galwall. He believed he possessed a calling to minister to the rural and remote folk of Australia.

Gina had held her father while he succumbed to a deadly snakebite. Her mother had tried in vain to raise the air ambulance on their obstinate and fickle UHF radio. Desperately she had tried, as Gina watched the life force that was her father slip away.

Gina's family, particularly her mother, lost a great deal when Gina was plucked from its bosom into the world of modelling at the age of fifteen. In the same year Audrey lost her husband, she also lost Gina—her household manager, her responsible child, her confidante—to a stranger who had merely taken the wrong road.

Most of all, Audrey's fear for Gina and her potential loss of innocence negated the woman's ability to envisage any good from an opportunity offered by a stranger.

Amid the party and despite the light banter, Gina could feel herself mentally slipping away. She excused herself, feigning a need to go to the bathroom. She closed the door on the familiar din and observed the older woman who looked back at her from the mirror. How did that happen, where did the years go? She sat on the loo for some time. Her head was supported in her hands like a swollen melon devoid of its vine. The thoughts that had crept into her consciousness intermittently over the past few months now blasted their way into the limelight. She knew what she must do. She also knew the condemnation and ridicule her decision would bring.

Chapter Two

"Hoy, Gina, you in there?" called Alexa, again interrupting her thoughts.

"Be out in a minute."

"My God, kiddo, I thought you'd been flushed into the Yarra. What the hell's going on in there—you got the trots?"

Gina knew she could no longer defer the inevitable and came out to meet Alexa in the wash area. "Alexa, I'm going to resign."

Alexa beamed. "'Bout fuckin' time you told them to stick it up their arse. I trust this means you're coming to work for me?"

"No, I'm going to become a remote area nurse."

Alexa burst into laughter, reeling back against the black marble wash basin. She laughed so hard she had to hold her stomach, and tears rolled down her cheeks. Gina felt the whole world was laughing as the wide expanse of mirror reflected Alexa's hilarity. Eventually Alexa regained enough composure to speak. "A fuckin' what? You've come up with some harebrained ideas since I've known you, but this definitely takes the cake. How long you been bakin' this one?" She resumed her mirth. "Bullshit, Gina. Pull the other one. I've never heard anything so ridiculous. Do you know what a pittance nurses earn? They work disgusting hours and perform even more disgusting tasks. You *are* kidding?" asked Alexa gingerly.

Gina washed her hands and slowly turned to Alexa, her composure surprisingly intact. She had correctly anticipated Alexa's reaction and was well prepared. "No, I'm not. I've given it a lot of thought over a long period—ever since I was a young girl, actually—and for some reason which at this moment I can't quite explain, this is something I must do."

Alexa looked at her quizzically and sobered. "You're serious, aren't you … Do you realise the amount of study you're going to have to do? It'll take years. What does Savannah think about this midlife crisis decision?"

Alexa drew breath, enabling Gina to infiltrate the inquisition. "I haven't discussed it with her yet, but she will have a number of options. It will be quite a few years before I would be leaving to take up a position. She'll be almost a grown woman by the time I've finished study and placements."

An exasperated Alexa then launched into another barrage of questions. "And go to uni for what, three or four years, with a group of poxy, hormone-ravaged eighteen-year-olds? Give up your job, status, and income to be treated like crap by a lot of frustrated old maids with a white shoe fixation? You'll be the lowest of the low in the health food chain—almost worse off than a female recruit in the army."

"It will be four years at uni, because I want to study midwifery after I complete a health science degree. All in all, it will take at least five or six years, as I will also need to do a year's clinical experience before I can start midwifery. And you know something? I too will be hormone ravaged but at the opposite end of the bleeding cycle. It will make an interesting combination, don't you think?" Gina raised a questioning eyebrow and awaited Alexa's comeback.

"Yeah sure, why don't you write about it? It'll make a good story," Alexa scoffed. She then looked at Gina and her face softened. "Maybe you've already hit the craziness of the change. I think you're fucked in the head, my love, but you know I'll support you. Jeez, we should both live long enough to see you graduate!" Alexa redoubled her laughter.

Gina embraced her, tears brimming in her eyes as she thanked her dear friend. She had known that Alexa would not disappoint her—she never had. They hugged for a prolonged moment, both aware that their friendship was about to change irrevocably. They would miss the camaraderie they'd shared since their first meeting ten years ago. But their relationship would endure.

Now to face the rest of the world.

Leaving her job was tinged with some sadness and lots of doubt. Gina was admonished by most of her disbelieving colleagues, especially her boss, Geoff Thomas. He could not comprehend why anyone in their right mind would even contemplate such a move.

Of greatest surprise to Gina was the support of her ex-husband, Aiden. He said he had always sensed her circle was not complete and knew that it was something bigger than their relationship. Aiden not only verbalised his support but was very understanding of Savannah's negative reaction, which was fuelled by the opinions of her privileged private-school friends. They considered her mother's reduction in status to be demeaning. Aiden helped Savannah deal with this teenage crisis and encouraged her to be proud of her mother. He also took more responsibility for assisting with Savannah's various commitments—school, singing, and dancing.

His years of expert womanising were put to good use as he coerced Savannah into acceptance. Savannah loved and respected her father. Fortunately for her, Gina and Aiden had never spoken ill of each other in her presence. Sadly, the good looks that had aided his womanising were becoming harder to distinguish. His dark brown hair was greying and disappearing. A shiny dome now completed his elongated face. A line of grey hair trailed from just above one ear around the back of his head to the other ear. His height and carriage still lent him a look of distinction, which was somewhat spoiled by the beginnings of a middle-age spread.

Chapter Three

The years Gina and Aiden spent together had been full of love, laughter, and adventure. It was the adventure that held them together beyond an indeterminate point of deterioration. Aiden's journalism had complemented Gina's modelling career very well. They had travelled the world to the exotic, the wealthy, the poor, the simple, and the complicated.

Savannah had come into the world uninvited. Neither Gina nor Aiden were ready to sacrifice their life. Travelling the world enriched by the excitement of rubbing shoulders with the rich and famous was intoxicating and addictive. Gina carried a dichotomy of guilt: a woman not ready for a child and at the same time holding a palpable fear of losing her baby. She felt undeserving because of her ungrateful response to this precious gift of new life. These feelings were exacerbated by the rapidity with which Aiden accepted the thought of parenthood. Although Aiden's initial reaction was one of disbelief, he quickly realised it was because Gina had previously told him she was infertile due to an infection she had suffered during her teenage years. Aiden was perplexed by Gina's contradictory reaction.

Unknown to Aiden, Gina had already travelled this road. As an aspiring model, she had become pregnant by a photographer whom she later realised had screwed his way through many a photo shoot. Gina, in her innocence, had loved him deeply. Her naiveté had left her vulnerable to predators like Sean Burgen.

She had dreamed the dream of many of his conquests, believing he would be pleased to share her life and the parenting of their child.

She was very wrong: his reaction was one of disgust and anger. Sean accused her of trapping him. He denied paternity even though Gina knew there was no other possibility.

Their son was born before his presence in the world was known. Like a ripple on a pond, her little boy had vanished, remembered only by Gina. It was while on location in the deserts of central Australia that Gina miscarried of a perfectly formed little boy. And it was here that Gina re-encountered Aboriginal people in their homelands. In broken English, the women of dark skin and poignant black eyes conveyed their compassion and support, empathetically mothering her while she awaited air transport evacuation. They conveyed a universal nurturing that transcended language. In their firm but gently persuasive manner, they insisted Gina hold her son, cry for him, cuddle him, and say goodbye to him.

Gina was forever grateful for those precious, intimate, and private moments. These women had known she must have this time alone. Through maturing eyes, Gina came to realise the plight of indigenous people and how the bureaucracy had failed these gentle souls. It was these women whose unquestioning acceptance soothed her spirit and made those precious moments with her son so real for her.

Many years later, she mentioned her miscarriage to Alexa but never spoke of the comfort she had found with her indigenous sisters or of the sadness that remained. It had felt too personal, too precious to be shared, and still aroused overwhelming guilt.

Due to the rains, Gina had waited three days to be evacuated to the Alice Springs hospital, by which time she was suffering a major pelvic infection. She was later informed by an officious young doctor that she would probably never conceive another baby. She had simply chosen to omit the preliminary details and had told Aiden only of the infection and its consequences. Up until the time of Savannah's conception, three years after her marriage, she had not used any form of contraception. In her mind, this had surely confirmed the doctor's edict.

Gina remembered well the day her world as she knew it came to an end. Years later, while she and Aiden were working in Rome, an Italian doctor informed Gina that her tiredness and nausea were not caused, as she had surmised, by overwork or anaemia, but by a little bambino. Since that announcement, Gina had many times relived her initial reaction of tears, closely followed by laughter and a kaleidoscope of emotions.

The pregnancy had initially been difficult. Physically she remained well. Emotionally she endured a six -month roller coaster, unable to come to terms with her thoughts and feelings about the enforced changes to her life. It was different for Aiden, she often mused. His life would alter very little, and he welcomed the idea of a baby in their lives. Why shouldn't he? He would continue to do what he had always done. A pregnancy would not change his body shape; it wouldn't jeopardise his career. It wouldn't entail his breasts producing a substance that was foreign to him, so that he felt akin to a Jersey cow. His life would continue unabated.

Gina resented Aiden's excitement about parenthood. Underlying these thoughts was her inability to accept that this baby was growing normally and would be born healthy. She had long ago resigned herself to the fact that motherhood was not an option. She would not allow herself to get too close to *this* unborn and uninvited child.

It wasn't until the flutters within her became undeniable that the stirrings of motherly anticipation impacted her psyche. Slowly Gina began to respond to the little person growing inside her. She began to assimilate this person as part of her but at the same time separate from her. She began to share special moments with her little person— moments only she could experience. They both danced to the sounds of "Smokie" while Gina sang, or relaxed to the Mozart's Symphony No. 6. They enjoyed the soothing touch of massage as Gina encircled her expanding bump with lavender-oiled palms and explained the wonders of the world her child would soon experience.

Aiden was an attentive expectant father. He was exhilarated by the feel of his child's movements and the idea of the woman he loved nurturing and finally giving birth to their baby.

The miracle of birth transformed them both. They fell in love with each other and with their beautiful daughter. After a small protest at being evicted from the warmth and safety of her mother, their beautiful creation looked in wide-eyed wonderment at her doting parents. She was a delight from that moment onwards. Gina and Aiden loved her deeply and enjoyed the first four years of her life, besotted by her as she explored her world.

They decided to continue their lives much as they had done. Savannah became an international baby. The physical effects on Gina were far less than she'd feared. Motherhood was certainly challenging, but with Aiden's devotion and assistance, life soon regained its former pace. Gina found life was enriched by Savannah's presence. Before the tender age of three, the baby had been to Japan, Vietnam, southern Europe, America, and Great Britain. She travelled well, contented just to be in the presence of either of her parents, sensing their love and inclusion.

Gina couldn't determine an exact moment when things began to sour between her and Aiden. It was probably during Savannah's fifth year of life. In fairness to Aiden, Gina admitted that the other women in his life had followed rather than caused their drifting apart. Their rift widened when they decided to curb their travelling and settle back in Melbourne. No longer could the excitement of wandering sublimate the shortcomings of their relationship. Their life directions had bifurcated, and neither seemed able to compromise sufficiently to meet the other's needs.

Gina often pondered the demise of their relationship. She was saddened by its fate but heartened by their lasting amity and sharing of parental responsibility. Above all, she was grateful their happier years had resulted in the birth of their beloved Savannah.

Chapter Four

Gina found her studies much more challenging than she had expected. Trying to remember the names of body parts, the systems to which they belonged, and how those systems worked was difficult enough. Having not been to school for over twenty years, she found the science and maths subjects particularly difficult. Fortunately for her Gina was financially secure and able to employ tutors to assist along the rocky road to graduation. What kept her going was that she enjoyed the clinical placements very much, especially her work experience in community health and paediatrics. The final placement in the third year of her degree was in a remote Aboriginal community near Alice Springs. It was this placement that confirmed her desire to work in a remote area, as her father before her.

University days were not without joy. Although Gina felt like a fish out of water initially, the younger students readily accepted her. She became mother confessor to many in the group and enjoyed her time with her younger colleagues. Being privy to their thoughts and feelings made it easier for her to understand the challenges Savannah was beginning to face.

Gina became a good student, much to her own surprise. What she lacked in knowledge of the sciences, she more than compensated for through motivation, life experience, and application to her work. Her reward was to gain first place in her favourite subject: family and community health.

Graduation day was celebrated in true celebrity style. The mistake Gina made was allowing Alexa to take charge of the proceedings. She invited just about the whole fashion mag industry. Gina was sure that many of them came just to verify for themselves that she had actually done it—she was now able to register as a nurse with the Victorian Nurses Board. Savannah, Alexa, and Aiden attended the formal ceremony. They were very proud companions at her graduation. She knew also that her mum and dad were with her in spirit. Gina was proud of her achievement.

The Royal Princeton Hospital was the first to employ Gina as a registered nurse. Her first day on the ward was a nightmare; she seriously contemplated resigning. Caring for seven very ill patients alone was a shock after caring for the one or two patients she had been allocated during clinical placements, and then under the watchful eye of a tutor. Her feet and legs ached and her head throbbed. Tiredness swallowed her like a fog on the moors. She slept fitfully, waking frequently to question whether she had completed and recorded various tasks. She couldn't believe how exhausted she was—maybe she was not cut out for nursing after all, or maybe she was simply too old.

The year passed rapidly. Her entry into midwifery heralded a return to the books and some semblance of a sane life with minimal shift work. *It shouldn't be too bad*, thought Gina. She was ready for study after her year away from university. She had almost grown to miss uni life and the assignment deadlines.

How wrong one could be. Midwifery turned her concept of nursing upside down. She had to learn to be rather than to do. She had to change her thinking from an illness model to a wellness model, yet be forever vigilant for potential problems. Pregnancy was, after all, a normal life event for a healthy woman. Birthing a baby was not, they were taught, a medical achievement. Birth was an accomplishment belonging to the woman—under normal circumstances only she could birth her baby.

The dichotomy of this learning troubled Gina. What she learned in midwifery lectures varied greatly from the highly technical, disempowering medical births she had witnessed during the clinical placements. Clinical placements for midwifery included being assigned to birthing suites in two major training hospitals.

Prior to completing her midwifery course, Gina applied for several jobs in remote areas. It was late in June before Gina received a positive response from any of the three applications. She would complete her course mid-year and hoped to have a position by then.

She and Savannah had discussed Savannah's options. To Gina's amazement, Savannah was quite determined to join her when she took up a position. Gina had been sure Savannah would want to stay at college with her friends and complete her schooling. She felt equally sure that Savannah would hate living in such remote and basic circumstances. Aiden was more than happy to have Savannah live with him. Even though Gina did not need the financial assistance, he had also offered to pay half Savannah's airfare should she want to visit her mum during the holidays. Gina was surprised and delighted by his support and generosity. She surmised that she and Aiden made a better friend than a marriage partner.

Gina had often mused over her feelings in relation to Savannah. She felt a growing sadness that began to sow the seeds of doubt. She and Savannah had been inseparable. Gina's decision to take a desk job with a magazine had been made largely because she wanted to maintain an ordered and secure life for Savannah—one Gina knew she couldn't achieve in the out-front modelling world. Outwardly she discouraged Savannah from joining her now. Inwardly she hoped Savannah *would* join her, that Savannah would be able to cope with a humble existence and being away from her friends. Gina knew this was selfish but also felt deep down that it had the potential to be a most enlightening period of personal growth.

Finally, a positive response arrived one week prior to the completion of her midwifery course—crunch time. Carmen Ashdown, chief nurse for the East Arnhem Region, Northern Territory, phoned her. They were desperate for a nurse to go to Lumbarta Island as soon as possible. Lumbarta Island was situated one hundred kilometres off the East Arnhem coast in the Gulf of Carpentaria. It was home to a thriving prawning industry. Approximately one thousand Aboriginal people, or "black fellas," and about thirty to forty "white fellas" lived there on a permanent or seasonal basis. The white fellas consisted mainly of teachers, pilots, police, maintenance workers, and health personnel. Prawning workers were transients, Carmen explained, who only stayed on the island during the prawn season. The sole township was built at the junction of the river mouth and the ocean, although one Aboriginal group lived on an outstation at the top end of the island. A doctor from Gove—or Nhulunbuy, its Aboriginal name—visited once a week.

It would of course be necessary for Gina to spend a few months at Nhulunbuy Hospital to gain some remote area experience and learn cultural mores. All patients requiring ongoing or urgent medical treatment, and pregnant women in their last trimester were flown to Nhulunbuy for care. The clinic on Lumbarta Island provided only day-to-day care between the hours of 0900 and 1700. She would be working with three experienced Aboriginal health workers and one trainee. She would be required to share after hours on call with them.

Carmen went into detail about the living arrangements. "The accommodation on the island is air conditioned but basic—a second-rate, motel-sized bathroom and toilet, a single bed, a small lounge and eating area, a kitchenette, and a veranda enclosed by wire mesh. It's one of a block of three health department flats—the other two are made available for overnight health visitors. There is one vehicle attached to the clinic—a four-wheel-drive Nissan referred to as 'the truck.' A store on the island sells most essentials and a limited array of groceries. Fresh fruit is flown in each week, and other supplies are delivered by barge once a month."

Carmen advised that an interview wouldn't be necessary. Gina could come up on three months' trial to see if "they liked each other." After the probation period, Gina's airfare would be reimbursed.

The weeks before Gina's departure were crazy. Savannah, at the gentle persuasion of both her parents, elected to stay with her dad until she'd completed her school year—year 11. She then wanted to live with Gina and complete year 12 via correspondence. Neither Gina nor Aiden thought this was a wise choice but doubted that Savannah would survive in the Territory for long. Just in case, Gina had negotiated with Carmen for Savannah to reside in one of the flats.

Gina's Melbourne flat was let. As Gina packed up their personal belongings, she began to feel quite melancholy and question the wisdom of her decision. She donated most of her clothes to the women's shelter in the knowledge that her glamorous wardrobe would be both superfluous in the tropics but also to many of the women at the shelter.

Carmen was a short, thin woman who spoke at a million miles an hour and possessed a lively sense of humour. She had dark brown, lifeless hair that was tidy but not stylish, as were her clothes—a symptom of being just too busy to attend to her appearance, Gina decided. After the formality of the hierarchy at her training hospitals, Gina found Carmen's informality and collegiality refreshing. She instantly liked Carmen and that rapport was mutual.

She and Carmen were similar in age and had much in common. Carmen warned Gina that nursing at Nhulunbuy Hospital was very different from nursing in a large metropolitan hospital—it required a much higher degree of responsibility and autonomous decision making.

The hospital's patients were largely Aboriginal. Women were transported from their homelands around the top end to birth in hospital. The system allowed a local caregiver known as a doula to accompany a pregnant woman during labour and birth. Doulas generally spoke little. When they did speak, it was in their tribal tongue. Their presence was a great comfort to the women, who laboured silently and valiantly.

Gina was dismayed that some of the women "absconded" back to their homeland prior to their due date. It took some time for her to understand that the idea of giving birth away from their homelands was unacceptable to these women.

She thrived on the autonomy of nursing at Nhulunbuy. At the same time, she was comforted by having medical staff readily available, especially when attending births. Indigenous women were encouraged to listen to their bodies and surrender to the birthing process. Unless the midwife was concerned, doctors did not routinely become involved in this aspect of "women's business." As a new midwife, Gina gained immeasurable experience and confidence.

Gina had worked for only a month at Nhulunbuy Hospital when Carmen summoned her to the office. Carmen explained that they were desperate to have her take up the position on Lumbarta Island, as the previous incumbent had resigned without notice. She wondered if Gina, who was more mature than their usual candidates, felt ready to take on this challenge.

Gina was excited and terrified—working alone, without skilled medical assistance, and in an isolated community would be a challenge. However, she couldn't wait and said she was happy to take the next flight out. The next morning, Gina packed up her now meagre belongings and headed for the airport to catch the island plane.

Gina struggled with her luggage and was directed, unaided and unchecked, from the small airport building across the boiling black tarmac to the island plane. The closer she got to the plane, the higher her anxiety level rose. She detected a smug smile on the lips of the young man whom she presumed to be the pilot. Despite his uniform confirming his credentials, he looked like he should still be in school.

"Hi, I'm Marc Bradshaw, at your service. So you're the new nurse? Welcome to the Lumbarta Express. I'm so glad to see we have the original Florence Nightingale joining us." He smirked as he nodded toward the small lamp Gina was hugging protectively.

The lamp was Gina's one symbol of home—a precious possession she had safely transhipped. She had salvaged it from her mother's scant belongings. She was not about to leave it behind. It was a small, white-frosted, glass-domed lamp with an ornamental brass stand and base. Around the white dome was a delicate crystal- and pearl-beaded fringe that tinkled in the crosswind that swept red dust across the tarmac.

Gina instantly liked this cheerful young man and couldn't help but wonder about her firstborn. Would he be about Marc's age if he'd survived?

"Thank you. I'm Gina Atkins, and yes, the grapevine is working well. Are you implying that I am like the original Florence Nightingale because of my age or the lamp? I'll have you know, young man, that this is an advanced model—it runs on *electricity*. And I might say that nursing knowledge has also advanced since Florence's era."

Marc let out a bemused sigh, accompanied by a disarming smile. "Sorry, no disrespect intended. I look forward to your modern ministrations, ma'am."

Gina was both embarrassed and somewhat flattered by Marc's subtle innuendo. Dressed in her travelling clothes, she still commanded a second look. Her beige shorts and white, crisply ironed, button-up blouse highlighted a well-preserved figure. Her hair was swept up and held softly in place by large white combs. Marc couldn't help but wonder about her choice of colours. Nothing stayed white on the island, but he guessed she'd learn that soon enough.

When Gina perused the butter box with wings on which they were about to board, her sense of adventure was tested. She said a little prayer to her guardian angels for assistance as she climbed the flimsy steps into the tiny cabin of the plane.

The flight was bumpy over the gulf waters, and Gina was sure she was going to throw up. She was seated up front next to Marc, and he took account of her slowly fading complexion. "First flight in a small plane?" he yelled over the engine noise.

She just nodded, terrified to open her mouth for fear more than words would flow from it.

"OK. Relax. Let those tense tummy muscles go and breathe deeply. Holding your tummy tense won't really help keep the plane in the air; it will just increase your nausea."

Gina glared at him for skilfully and accurately exposing her disposition.

"That's great. I can see the colour returning to your face already," he lied.

It was hot in the plane, and the smells of avgas and body odour, combined with the heat, were not helping her constitution. Gina was the one and only passenger.

"You may want to open that window a bit further—get some more air. We're soon coming down to land."

Thank God, thought Gina as her stomach continued to do cartwheels.

"I will buzz the health centre to let them know we've arrived. As I circle the airstrip and descend, it may get a bit uncomfortable," warned Marc.

She couldn't imagine it getting any worse. Then she caught a glimpse of a knowing and amused look from Marc. She felt too ill to admonish his insolence.

Leaving her high-profile position as fashion editor of *Women's Love* to follow this path had been, as many of her colleagues had told her, sheer madness. She now yearned for her large air-conditioned office and the sweet smell of fresh roses that adorned her desk each week, compliments of the management.

Deep down, however, beyond her nausea, she knew it was much more than a whim that had brought her to this remote part of Australia. It had required deep conviction, a lot of hard work, determination, and, as Alexa had so aptly described it, "the sheer bloody grit of a lunatic."

Chapter Five

Gina wondered if heralding their arrival by buzzing the clinic had had the desired effect. Carmen had assured her that someone would collect her.

The rising red dust cloud heralded an approaching vehicle. She and Marc were showered in red grit as "the truck" hurtled towards them, then came to an abrupt halt. The dust settled to unveil a young Aboriginal man jumping out of the driver's seat. He greeted Marc warmly. "Hey, bro—this blood to go to hospital in Nhulunbuy." His smile engulfed his delightfully friendly face, ivory teeth, and twinkling eyes. His beautiful dark-brown skin was surrounded by a mass of black curls, in his beard and on his head. He was of medium height, his head level with Marc's shoulders.

The young escort did not make eye contact with Gina and referred to her as if she was not present. "This Sister Gina, nah?"

"Yoh," said Marc, nodding.

"I'm Yarunda, sexual health worker. Jalnu, head health worker, send me to fetch you," he announced proudly, looking at Gina for the first time.

Gina estimated Yarunda to be in his early to mid-thirties, although she found it difficult to accurately estimate the ages of these richly coloured East Arnhem Land people—their dark skin seemed to belie their years. Yarunda was wiry thin. His smile suggested a pleasant, relaxed disposition.

Gina extended her hand, which Yarunda took gingerly. "Hallo,

Yarunda. Yes, I'm Gina Atkins, the new nurse. Thank you for coming to collect me."

Yarunda beamed and waved goodbye to Marc.

Marc called out as Gina and Yarunda loaded her well-travelled and incongruously elegant luggage into the Nissan. "See you round. Wade Porter and I are the two pilots currently based on the island, so we'll probably run into each other a bit. Us white fellas have an occasional get-together on the island– invite the chalkies, cops, grease monkeys, and any other stray white trash over for the occasional barbie." Marc grabbed the esky containing the blood specimens and placed it into the small luggage compartment at the front of the plane. On command the engines roared into action. Marc taxied to the end of the strip and banked over the saltbush and disappeared. On board too was Gina's resolve.

Gina's growing trepidation was tempered by the thought of calling home. She couldn't wait to get to the clinic so she could phone Savannah and Alexa to let them know she'd arrived safely.

The trip into town was indeed an experience. The road consisted of rutted, red, compacted sand intermittently dotted with large potholes and bog holes of soft, powdery sand. The vegetation was sparse and mainly consisted of shrubs, which became non-existent as they reached the first dwellings on the outskirts of town.

The unfolding sights, sounds, and smells shocked Gina. Some dwellings were reasonably new, but many were no more than dilapidated collections of unpainted wooden boards and sheets of iron, hanging together to represent a house. The windows were framed holes in the wall, and not one side of the dwellings was parallel to its opposing wall. The entrance was merely that—few had doors. The stumps on which they stood looked like railway tracks and were as rusted as the iron roofs that provided a meagre degree of shelter.

It was almost evening, and the women were outside their houses, cooking on makeshift campfires. Kids ran everywhere, including into the path of the Nissan. Mostly, Gina noticed, people just sat. Men seemed to huddle in small groups, seemingly oblivious to her arrival or the raucous squeals of kids running between them. Women not involved in cooking also sat in groups, stealing curious looks as the truck passed by. The activity level of the adults was hard to discern and in sharp contrast to the energy exuded by the kids. A small group of men and women absorbed in a card game seemed slightly more animated. Gina was disturbed by the inactivity she observed but knew she had no business making early judgements of these people, on whose land she was a guest.

Amid what appeared to be pandemonium, Gina noticed the "leather dogs" to which Carmen had referred in her departure briefing. There seemed to be at least three or four at each camp. They were the skinniest, mangiest-looking creatures Gina had ever seen. They seemed to be wandering free: sniffing at cooking utensils, snarling at one another, and generally making themselves at home or relieving themselves wherever they chose. Gina shivered in disgust— this aspect of life she would find very difficult.

Much to Gina's amazement and relief, Yarunda deftly avoided the kids and slowed to allow the nonchalant leather dogs to meander across their path. He pointed out the council building and the town store, neither of which inspired confidence. Most of the official buildings in town were fibro with iron roofs, painted in colours that screamed at their surroundings. Gina pulled her lamp closer to her body, seeking reassurance.

Yarunda stopped in front of a rambling blue fibro building with a ramp leading to its front veranda. "This the clinic," he announced as he honked the horn. He jumped out of the Nissan and went to its rear door to retrieve Gina's bags. Two Aboriginal women came out of the clinic. One appeared to be quite young, about seventeen or eighteen. She was a very attractive young woman with a smile that melted Gina's apprehension.

"Allo, I'm Mandy, health worker in training. This is Donna—health worker." She motioned with a jut of her chin towards the other woman.

Gina estimated that Donna was probably in her mid-thirties. She had prominent yet attractive facial features and was, by local standards, well covered but not overweight. Her legs were typically thin. Donna greeted her cautiously but with a smile. "Allo, welcome to Lumbarta Island."

Gina responded with all the confidence and warmth she could muster, "Hello to you both. I'm very pleased to be here. If it's OK with you, I might have a quick look through the clinic, and we can catch up on other things tomorrow. I'm looking forward to working with you all."

Without further response, Donna began to walk away from Gina. She slightly twisted her hand and forearm as she did so. Gina stood still, awaiting further instruction. Donna stopped and again did the hand thing, which Gina then realised was a motion that meant "follow me."

Donna led her into the clinic. They walked through a labyrinth of areas and rooms, some obviously well used and others that looked like they hadn't been used in years. Gina thought the place was dirty but relatively tidy. She would quickly learn that keeping anything clean amid the red dust and sand was near impossible.

Gina noticed another woman standing in an internal office. She was a small, stout woman who had a gentle face and was dressed in a brightly patterned "zippy" dress. Donna and Mandy were also wearing zippy dresses, which Gina later learned were both cool and practical. The dresses were patterned in bold colours, they opened down the front via a zip, were sleeveless, and had a large pocket on each side. It wasn't long before Gina herself adopted this local fashion. She knew her ex-colleagues would have found it most amusing.

The woman in the office seemed to be eying Gina warily. She watched intently and unemotionally as they passed the glass partition between the office and the waiting area. At the end of their inspection tour, Donna led Gina to the office. Gina stood while Donna and the woman exchanged conversation in their native language. Though she guessed she was the topic of discussion, she had no idea what was said.

The woman then approached Gina. "I'm Jalnu, head health worker in charge. How long you staying?" she asked abruptly.

Gina was surprised by her question and its implication. She wasn't quite sure what Jalnu meant by it. She was, however, reasonably sure of the intent—she felt this woman was asserting her authority. Trying to appear calm, Gina replied, "Hallo, I'm Gina Atkins. It's a pleasure to meet you, Jalnu. Carmen Ashdown, the chief nurse, has told me many good things about you and how you have run this clinic so well."

Jalnu remained straight-faced and unmoved by her attempt at camaraderie. Gina felt she must tread carefully if she was to obtain the trust needed for them to work successfully with one another.

"Jalnu, I'm merely here to help with some of the more difficult tasks. I shall need to consult with you often, as I have many things to learn about your people and your community. The other health workers will report to you as the head health worker. I am here for you to talk with if problems arise that you feel you would like to discuss. We can look at many things together and how they are done. I might suggest other ways of doing them, but it's up to you whether we change anything. As for how long I am staying, I have no plans to leave. I hope, if you're happy with me and the community approves, that I can stay for a long time."

Jalnu shrugged her shoulders and resumed her work. She used her native tongue to issue further instructions to Donna. Gina was unprepared for this apparent rudeness and hesitantly ventured, "Do you think I could use the telephone just to let my daughter and my friend know that I've arrived safely?"

Jalnu scowled at her and again turned back to her work without further comment.

Donna burst into laughter and explained, "No telephone 'ere. Only council have satellite phone. We use radio to call Air Medical Service, nah."

Gina froze, not because there was no 'phone, but because her childhood memory of UHF radios was that the inefficiency of radio communication, she'd concluded, killed her father. She regained her composure.

"Oh my goodness, I didn't realise … I can't do that; this is not a medical call."

"It's after hours now, Sister Gina. They will relay messages or try to get your call for you. I show you."

Donna giggled as she called AMS and explained the situation. She handed the microphone to Gina.

"Welcome, Gina. This is Nancy in Darwin. We will no doubt speak often. Do you want to talk with your people, or do you want me to relay a message?"

Thank goodness, thought Gina, *a friendly white fella voice on the other end of the radio.* She suddenly felt isolated and lonely, hiding her near-tearful demeanour. "If it's not too much trouble, I'd love to speak with my daughter in Melbourne—Savannah Atkins."

She gave the number, and Nancy instructed her on radio etiquette: times she could make personal calls, how to say "over" at the end of each group of sentences, and how to finish with "over and out" so Nancy would know Gina had completed her conversation.

It was so good to hear Savannah's voice. At first their conversation was awkward as they became accustomed to the relay lag and waiting for the "over" before responding. Savannah asked Gina lots of questions, many of which Gina could not answer as truthfully or as descriptively as she'd have liked. All the health workers remained in the office to hear and watch. Moreover, Gina soon realised that her audience also included the whole of the radio network throughout the Territory.

Savannah chatted mainly about school and said she couldn't wait until next January, when she would be coming up. Gina explained that they were using an AMS frequency, so they had to keep it short. She promised to write soon. She was suddenly very homesick and tried to hide her discomfort. Jalnu had not missed this and looked at her disdainfully.

"Come," Donna said, motioning with her chin for Gina to follow. "I'll take you to the flat."

Donna grabbed a key from a wall hook. Gina collected her bags in preparation to follow. She struggled a little with her bags and lamp. There was no attempt by Donna to assist her. She was conscious again of Jalnu eyeing her through the glass partition. The woman's gaze seemed fixed on the lamp, a sceptical eyebrow appearing to question Gina's sanity.

They left the clinic via the back door. She followed Donna along a narrow path and down a small hill to another blue building. The three flats were built one story off the ground and had a common laundry on the ground floor. The truck was parked underneath. Carmen's description of the flat proved to be accurate. Dealing with the reality of living in such a small dwelling would take some adjustment. The only positive aspect Carmen had omitted was the lovely view from the front veranda. It was narrow but overlooked the beach. Gina was grateful for the gentle afternoon sea breeze that wafted through its mesh walls.

"It's been a very long day and I'm beat," she said. "If it's OK with you, I'll settle in and unpack my belongings and have something to eat before I fall into bed."

"Yah, yah, see you in the morning. Eight thirty sharp, OK? Jalnu will get very cross if you're late. Maybe she will take you to meet the town president. Don't forget, keep your security doors locked—some rascals are about, sometimes sniffing bad."

Gina smiled and decided not to question Donna's warning more closely. She'd leave that for another day. "Thank you, and thanks for the warning. I'll look forward to tomorrow. Goodnight, Donna."

Gina surveyed her surroundings—Carmen's comparison to a second-rate motel room was apt. The contents of the flat were basic but adequate. There had been no attempt to prepare for her arrival. The bed was unmade, there were no supplies apart from those Gina had brought with her, and red dust had settled on every visible surface. The dull mustard-coloured decor, uncoordinated curtains, and stark linoleum floor darkened her already sensitive mood. The bathroom had a tiled floor and laminate walls. The tiles were also mustard in colour, many were cracked or chipped. Mould filled the chips and plugged the cracked grout. The walls were a patterned grey from an era past—in all, a decorator's nightmare. To bring her comfort, she plugged in her precious lamp and turned it on. She then sat on the stained, dusty mattress and cried.

Chapter Six

Whether it was the light or heat that woke Gina, she was unsure. It was four thirty in the morning. Her damp hair seemed to be matted to her pillow, and her nightshirt stuck like a second skin. She vowed she would never again go to sleep without her fan turned on and her nightshirt off. Fortunately, the exhaustive state that finally overtook her tears ensured a sound sleep. The sunlight streaming through the front windows slightly buoyed her somewhat fragmented but renewed feelings of excitement and anticipation.

Gina's first week on the job was mentally and physically taxing. In addition to the long days at the clinic, she was also on call at least two nights per week or one night and the weekend. She quickly learned a little of the many and varied family configurations. "Poison relatives" were a new concept. Some interactions were taboo in Aboriginal culture. Mandy suddenly sprinted out the rear door of the clinic when her poison uncle appeared on the front veranda, refusing to come in to have his dressing attended, until Mandy disappeared. After-hours complaints ranged from headaches, to fevers, to spear wounds to petrol-sniffing psychosis. She now understood Donna's reference to sniffing on her first night, but had no idea of the extreme impact it had on the user and the community.

She had so much to learn. Little in her nursing experience had prepared her for the multitude and range of complaints these people suffered. She soon worked out that conventional treatments were useless in many instances. Most infections were treated by antibiotic injections; oral antibiotics were rarely administered. There were many reasons for apparent non-compliance in taking oral antibiotics—many patients did not understand the concept of germs and chose to present to the clinic only when their infections reached an acute and incapacitating stage. Once they began to feel better, they no longer perceived a need to continue treatment. Very few had suitable safe and cool places to store medication. Scheduling regular medication times was futile for a people driven by need and not clocks.

To Gina's surprise, much of Yarunda's work simulated that of a detective. In his efforts to ensure a course of treatment was followed and to find the contacts of patients infected by sexually transmitted diseases, he drove around in the truck, asking after people's whereabouts. He stopped them where he found them, collecting blood from some and giving injections of antibiotics to others. This very public treatment of a very private condition fazed no one except Gina, who soon realised that the lack of confidentiality engendered by such methods was her problem alone.

What made life more taxing was the attitude of Jalnu. Gina tried daily to win her confidence but to no avail. She was perplexed and troubled by her inability to strike up meaningful communication and a feeling of camaraderie. She knew it was imperative if they were to work successfully together. By the end of the second week, Gina decided there was little more she could do. She would try to work around the issue, although this would be difficult given the high esteem in which Jalnu was held by the other health workers and the community.

On Tuesday of the third week, Jalnu motioned for Gina to follow her. Jalnu offered no explanation, and Gina thought it better not to ask—*Patience*, she told herself. They had been in the middle of a particularly busy clinic. It was "doctor's day" and the first time she was working with Doctor David Peters in the community. She had briefly met his acquaintance at Nhulunbuy Hospital.

David Peters was about forty years old, with rugged good looks and wavy blonde hair. His dress was casual: faded blue shorts and a cream checked shirt unbuttoned to his nipple line. His footwear consisted of brown leather sandals which housed his muscly tanned legs. His medical prowess was reassuring, but his manner towards Gina was offhand. Paradoxically, he was inclusive, patient, and educative when working with the health workers. He was, to Gina's surprise, only mildly irritated when she told him she must leave him for a short time at Jalnu's insistence. It appeared Jalnu had already given Dr David an explanation.

David was one of the few stayers in the region, with six years' remote experience to his credit. He understood the Aboriginal people, the importance of women's business, and the need to show respect to Jalnu as he treated her people. He also understood that some members of the community were not permitted to talk with others. He had no qualms about visiting poison relations in their homes. Gina thought David Peters was a difficult character, although the community obviously loved and trusted him.

Hurrying along in Jalnu's wake, Gina headed up the road towards the council building. Attempting to engage Jalnu in conversation, Gina commented on the activities of the people as they passed by. "It's interesting to see many people squat for so long." When no response was forthcoming, she ventured, "What is it they do? Is it that it's too hot to move around during the day, and they save the work till night?"

"Work! Humbug." Jalnu retorted and increased her pace, leaving Gina scurrying to catch up.

Upon their arrival at the council building, Jalnu announced their mission to the receptionist. The town clerk came in from an adjoining office and stood for some seconds, sizing up the newest recruit. When he motioned an acknowledgement with his jutting chin, Jalnu stood to introduce Gina. "This Karundi, he the town clerk. He pays the health workers through the community assistance scheme."

Karundi was a fat little man, unlike any of the community people Gina had encountered to date. His facial features depicted mixed blood: his shifty eyes were slightly angled, and his lips and nose were finer than those of most of the residents. The sallow brown of his skin supported Gina's assessment of him as having mixed Asian blood. He was much lighter in colour than that of most of the Lumbarta Islanders.

Jalnu turned to Gina and motioned. "This is Sister Gina. She the new nurse."

Gina extended her hand to Karundi. He ignored it. He grunted an unrecognisable response, then returned to his office.

Jalnu seemed unfazed by Karundi's rudeness. Gina found him quite unsettling. She became aware of her rising apprehension as their wait extended. It was twenty-five minutes before the receptionist announced that the president was ready to see them—time, Gina thought, that could have been better spent at the clinic. They were directed down a short, narrow, and dimly lit corridor. Jalnu knocked timidly at the office door, an action Gina found even more unnerving. Jalnu was a respected elder of the community and normally afraid of no one.

The door opened, and Gina found herself transfixed, barely able to respond to this man's unexpectedly gregarious greeting. His presence was awesome, and Gina could see why his community revered him.

Mandabartawarra was the tallest Aboriginal man Gina had met. He was slim and very dark-skinned. His plentiful greying hair tumbled in curls over his temples, his forehead, and the nape of his neck. His stately stature almost seemed incongruous with his friendly manner. He shook Gina's hand gently and firmly. "Sister Gina, my people speak well of you. Please accept my apologies for your long wait. I was detained by a phone call. I welcome you to our community and thank you for coming to help care for my people."

Gina was overwhelmed by his sincerity along with his educated application of the English language. She was also poignantly aware that the personal qualities, good looks, and poise that had improved her position in her former career were neither acknowledged nor necessary to earn this man's respect—they were, to her amusement, irrelevant. It was her acceptance by his people that mattered most. Her genuine concern had obviously come to his attention.

"It is I who must thank you for allowing me the privilege of working with your people," she replied. "They have been nothing but friendly and respectful. I am fortunate indeed to work alongside your experienced health workers and to have a leader such as Jalnu to show me your ways. Jalnu has been very patient with me, and I don't know how I would have managed without her."

Mandabartawarra beamed a smile of acknowledgement towards Jalnu. "Jalnu is a great leader. You are right; our community is indeed fortunate to have her as our senior health worker."

Jalnu's response surprised Gina. She became coy, bowed her head, and chuckled quietly, clearly embarrassed by Mandabartawarra's praise. Gina thought Jalnu also directed a smile at her. She realised her earlier interpretation of Jalnu's approach to Mandabartawarra was not derived out of intimidation or fear, rather reverence.

Mandabartawarra then asked, "Sister Gina, could you come and visit with me sometime soon? There are many issues about the health of my people that I would like to discuss with you."

Gina could hardly contain her excitement. "I would be delighted to talk with you. You are right, there are many health issues we could better deal with as a community. I would ask your permission to bring Jalnu to these discussions as I rely on her to direct the other health workers and give advice to your people."

"Of course, I'll look forward to it," said Mandabartawarra. He rose in a manner that indicated their meeting was over.

Gina and Jalnu hurried back to the clinic. Gina decided she would capitalise on the hint of warmth she'd detected from Jalnu and asked about Mandabartawarra. Jalnu explained that he had been educated by the missionaries and had shown extraordinary leadership and learning ability even as a boy. He had been sent to a church boarding school in Darwin to complete his education. Since his appointment as town president two years previously, he regularly flew to Darwin to attend the college, learn about managing communities, and meet with the government. His son had also attended boarding school in Darwin and now worked as a teacher's aide at the local school.

Shortly following her arrival on the island, the children had become Gina's primary concern. She found that many suffered with "school sores" and recurrent respiratory tract and ear infections. These same children were often anaemic and looked undernourished despite the abundance of seafood and bush tucker. Gina talked with the health workers about her concerns and learned that few in the community went without good food. Fish and kangaroo were common fare, as were local plants, berries, and legumes. There had to be other reasons for this pattern of ill health.

To investigate further Gina arranged a meeting through the school headmaster, Ian Turvey. She and Jalnu met with Ian, the two other teachers, and the teacher's aides. One of the teachers, a young woman named Sheree Montgomery, was particularly helpful and obviously shared Gina's concern for the health of her young charges. Also concerned were the two Aboriginal teacher's aides—Kiah, a friendly young woman about seventeen years old, and a young man, slightly older, who could be none other than Mandabartawarra's son. Balunn was a tall man whose strikingly handsome features surpassed those of his father. His laughing eyes glistened in the sunlight and centrifuged his engaging smile.

Balunn explained that while fresh food was plentiful, many students came to school without breakfast. Neither school nor breakfast was a cultural priority in the community. He suggested that they consider providing breakfast at school, as at boarding school. This would not only affect the children's health and their ability to concentrate, but would also entice many to come to school. He wondered if the poor state of the many dogs in town might have some connection with the children's health, because the dogs lived in such close proximity to their owners. He described the cooler months as being a one, two, or three-dog night depending on how many dogs were needed in one's bed to keep warm.

It was agreed that breakfast was an excellent suggestion. Balunn volunteered to assist with food preparation, provided the council could supply the food. Gina left the meeting with a resolve to approach the council and felt very pleased with their discussions. She was a little apprehensive at the prospect of speaking with Karundi on the matter and decided to take up the offer made by Mandabartawarra to meet separately.

During Dr Dave's next visit, Gina raised the issue of malnourishment and found David very receptive on the subject. "You know, Gina, I strongly suspect that we're looking at malnutrition as an effect and not a cause. Lack of suitable food is not so much a problem, but I strongly suspect that there is an association between ill health and the dogs."

"How's that?"

"Well, as you know, many of the kids who come to clinic are found to be anaemic. That's not due to their diet. It seems related to a widespread infestation by worms. The worms leech blood from the guts of the kids. The kids get worms because the dogs live in close quarters with the families and are themselves infected. The dogs not only roam free through the food preparation areas, as I'm sure you've noticed, but they sleep with the kids. It places the immune systems of the kids under constant siege and exacerbates the possibility for chest, skin, and ear infections."

"My goodness—this is much more complicated than I'd originally thought. What would you suggest?"

"Well, somehow we have to treat the community dogs. Before we do that, though, we'll have to have the cooperation of the community. Dogs are important to them."

"Yes. I discovered that the hard way when I nearly skittled one on my drive around town. Very scary! I guess the other issue is the control of dog numbers. None of them are spayed, and they just keep having puppies, which somehow survive despite the odds."

She rose to leave the room. Dr David looked up. "You're the first nurse since I've been coming here to show an interest in looking beyond the obvious. Keep looking for the causes instead of just treating the symptoms, and your work here will be rewarded tenfold. Good to have you on board."

Gina's heart soared—she considered this was probably a rare compliment and cherished it accordingly.

It was two weeks before Gina and Jalnu could secure an audience with Mandabartawarra to discuss the issue of child health. To Gina's delight, Balunn had pre-empted her visit, and Mandabartawarra readily agreed to subsidise breakfast at school. He said the council had already discussed this issue and were prepared to finance the project in the short term. He would draw up a proposal to put to the Northern Territory government for long-term funding under a plan for special projects in local communities.

When Gina explained the association between the dogs and diseases, Mandabartawarra saw the need to spay and de-infest the dogs. He agreed to apply for additional funding to engage a veterinary team, provided the owners of the dogs agreed. Some would still want puppies.

Mandabartawarra was officious but remained warm in dealing with this matter. He again rose to show Gina and Jalnu the door. As Jalnu left the office, Mandabartawarra called Gina back and shut the door. He turned to Gina, then hesitated. "Please, just one more minute of your time. Would you consider reviewing the proposal prior to my submitting it to the government? I want to be sure of the facts...and my sentence construction."

A little surprised but impressed by his forward thinking and willingness to ask for assistance, Gina smiled and nodded her consent, thrilled at being accorded such regard. She eventually managed to say, "I'd be honoured. Thank you."

"Just one more thing. How's it going at the clinic?"

"Really great!"

"Jalnu is a strong woman. She thinks much of you."

Gina found it difficult to hide her surprise at his knowledge and insight. She raised one eyebrow, a gesture not lost on Mandabartawarra. "You must understand that this community has been subjected to many and varied nurses over the past twelve months—thirteen in total. Some have caused my people no end of grief with their 'I know best' approach. Some have been culturally insensitive or have had inappropriate liaisons with Aboriginal men or women. We had one male nurse who was a drunkard and used to attend after-hours call-outs in an intoxicated state—not only a professional and moral misdemeanour, I'm sure you'll agree, but an insult to our community. This is a dry community, and the council has worked hard to keep it that way. Alcohol is not tolerated here. Sadly, remote communities often attract the undesirable 'white fella' element, and I think we've had more than our fair share."

"This explains a great deal. Thank you"

Gina took her leave of Mandabartawarra. She began to appreciate why he was a leader among men—quietly astute and inclusively decisive. He knew what Jalnu would be like with Gina. She finally understood that it was not Gina with whom Jalnu had an issue, but Gina's type. And in light of what had just been disclosed, who could blame her?

Chapter Seven

It was a hot summer Sunday morning. Gina sat on her small veranda, absorbing the scene before her. Flickering patterns from the golden sun reflecting on the ocean, changing constantly. The gentle breeze ensured that the white, sandy beach brought a new focus with each waft. It was truly beautiful.

Despite the privilege of being part of this splendour, Gina was feeling somewhat lonely. Donna was on call for the weekend. She had obviously coped well with any call-outs as she had not needed to contact Gina for support. Gina's thoughts were of her family and friends. It was two weeks before Christmas, and she knew her first Christmas away from Savannah would be very difficult. Her newfound chalkie friends would be leaving as soon as the school year was finished, to spend Christmas with their loved ones, as would most other white fellas who worked in the community. Only she, the local policeman Paul Russell, and his family would remain. The two pilots, Marc Bradshaw and Wade Porter, might do a run or two to the island over the festive season, but were unlikely to spend any time there. Although she had grown to love and respect these people, she was poignantly aware their cultures would remain divergent.

Savannah informed Gina and Aiden that she still intended to go to Lumbarta Island to live with Gina in the new year. She would complete her year 12 studies via correspondence. Gina and Aiden had both expressed their concern over this decision. Although Gina desperately wanted Savannah to experience her work and the people of this culture, she felt the timing was wrong. Up to year 11, Savannah had done well in all her subjects except for maths. Gina had concerns about how she would manage when the impetus for study had to come solely from self-motivation. Savanah would also miss her friends, social life and comforts.

Gina tried to explain to Savannah how basic life was on the island. Savannah merely said that she would then have more time for study.

In the end, Gina and Aiden agreed that Savannah could come to the island after Christmas and make her final decision just before school was due to resume. This would give her four weeks to sample life on the island. Both her parents were sure she would change her mind.

Gina was very much looking forward to spending those weeks with Savannah.

Tears began to course down Gina's cheeks as the loneliness consumed her. She felt sad but strangely contented, and knew deep down that this feeling would pass.

As if on cue, a knock at the back door of her flat startled her into the present. The bright, smiling face of Marc Bradshaw greeted her. "Hi, Gina—it's a great day for flying, and the coast guard have asked me to check out a reported sighting of an illegal fishing vessel in the bottom of the gulf. I was wondering if you're interested in a scenic flight. We can fly back over the lost city; you'll love it."

"Wow, am I. I was just feeling a bit lonely and sorry for myself. You are just what the doctor ordered. I'll be with you in two secs. Would you mind stopping at Donna's house for a minute? I need to let her know where I'll be."

"No probs," responded Marc.

Gina gathered her things and ran out to Marc's ute. He put the vehicle into drive, and it skipped and bounced over the rutted road to the airstrip.

"I hope your flying doesn't emulate your driving," Gina teased.

"No way. Didn't you know I'm the best of the best?" he retorted with the confidence of his youth.

Gina sat on an oil drum and watched as Marc pumped fuel from another drum into the tank. The plane danced on the airstrip, buffeted by the light breeze. It somehow seemed to share her excitement at the prospect of a non-routine flight. She wondered why she was about to entrust her life to such a rudimentary structure but was simultaneously aware of her building excitement. It would be wonderful to escape for a short time. She was thankful that the younger white women were out of town, as they no doubt would have taken precedence as suitable travelling companions. "Thank you so much for thinking of this lonely old lady. You've really brightened my day."

After Marc completed preliminary checks, the grinding motor roared at full throttle as they lifted off the runway. Almost immediately they were flying over picturesque swirls of sand banks and crystal blue-green waters, which soon melded into the deep blue of the ocean. They headed for the mainland coastline. Gina has never seen such a vast, beautiful, and unspoiled coastline. They seemed to fly forever along its pristine shores.

Gina was in awe of the sights unfolding before her. It was some time before she and Marc spoke. They scoured the coastline for signs of a possible rogue fishing vessel, but nothing came into view.

"What's the lost city? I didn't know there had ever been a city in these parts," Gina inquired.

Marc laughed. "No, there certainly has not to my knowledge. The lost city is a collection of rock formations that look like an ancient city. It is a sacred site of the Mungarra people. The Aboriginal elders conduct tours through the formations for the few off-road outback travellers who make it to these parts. Tourists are warned not to try to enter on their own, as it is easy to get lost. The black fellas say that some of the formations are taboo because they are occupied by bad spirits. We can't land there, but I can do a low flyover to give you an idea of how extensive and intricate the formations are."

"That would be fabulous. I would love to. This is wonderful!" exclaimed Gina.

Marc smiled as he manoeuvred the plane into a gentle dive, heading towards a distant rocky outcrop.

"I can see why it's called the lost city—the rock formations look too perfectly positioned to be natural," Gina observed.

"I've been on the tour and it sure is spooky. I wasn't sure whether it was our Mungarra guide and his superstitions that rubbed off on me or my own feelings and fears. but I was actually aware of the strangest presence of something," confided Marc.

Marc banked the plane and flew so low that Gina felt she could touch the sides of the rocky basin they entered. He was right: even from the air, she felt a sense of spirit that she couldn't begin to explain. She knew Marc would understand.

As she searched for the words to share her feelings, the radio crackled into life. "Victor, Bravo, Foxtrot, one niner eight—this is Air Med, Darwin. I have an urgent message for Gina Atkins. Over."

Gina steeled herself, wondering what travesty had constituted the need for a radio message.

"This is Victor, Bravo, Foxtrot, one niner eight—Marc Bradshaw speaking. I have Gina Atkins with me, and she has a set of phones on. Go ahead. Over."

"Gina, this is Nancy. I had a call from Donna at Lumbarta. She says that Old Man Nanderra, elder of the Curraba outstation, is having a heart attack. We have no way of getting him out. The Air Med plane cannot land there because the road is too narrow for our planes. It's a six-hour return trip by road. Donna wants to know what she should do. Over."

"Oh my God, let me think … I guess she'll have to drive up there. Tell her to take Yarunda with her and some oxygen and morphine, ten milligrams. We're heading back to Lumbarta Island now. Could you ask Nhulunbuy to despatch their Air Med plane? We will meet them at Lumbarta airstrip and wait for Donna and Yarunda to get back with the old man. Over."

"Hang on," interjected Marc. "I've flown up that way recently, and I think we might be able to land there if Donna could radio ahead and ask them to clear the road as best they can. It's worth a look. We could be there in half an hour. I carry oxygen on the plane. We could have him back to Lumbarta in time to meet the Nhulunbuy plane if it leaves now."

"Did you hear all that, Nancy? Over."

"Yes. I will get in touch with Nhulunbuy. Hey, don't take any chances, you two. It's not worth risking two lives to save one old man. Over."

"I agree, but this is one fit and very respected elder. I would like to give it a shot. Over and out," replied Gina.

The half-hour flight seemed to take forever. Gina felt very anxious, not only because they might be too late, but mostly because she had little equipment and fewer skills to help Nanderra.

Marc banked the plane and headed for what Gina thought was a bush track. As they neared, it broadened out for a short distance. It became apparent that this was where Marc intended to land. Off to the left stood a rusted and battered four-wheel-drive wagon with at least six pairs of arms waving out of the windows to them. Gina decided not to look during the final descent. Behind her tightly closed lids, she prayed they would land safely.

She felt the wheels touch down and pound along the coarse gravel road. They were quickly bundled into the wagon and headed towards the outstation. Gina grew more anxious as they approached the rudiments of civilization. The outstation consisted of a few tin shacks and lean-tos, campfires, and of course the mandatory leather dogs. She reflected on these mangy creatures who lived a scavenger's existence. They were walking skeletons, their thickened, hairless skin toughened to endure the sun's relentless rays.

They passed a remarkably clear waterhole where children swam and squealed in delight, unperturbed by the events unfolding around them. Gina admired their glistening brown bodies romping shamelessly naked in pursuit of fun.

She then caught sight of the old man sitting under a tree. Women elders were fussing around him. As they approached, she saw he was still very much alive, although he was clutching at his chest and his breathing was laboured—typical signs of a heart attack. He seemed to be agitated, motioning with his arm at his concerned carers.

Gina knelt-down beside him. She re-introduced herself and introduced Marc while simultaneously feeling for his pulse. She asked him about his chest pain.

Nanderra rubbed his chest and said, "It's all over—burning like fire."

Gina explained that she thought he might have suffered a heart attack and that they would need to fly him to Nhulunbuy straight away.

To her astonishment, Nanderra burst into laughter, embracing his chest and writhing with mirth. He spluttered, "Sister Gina, you *give* old man a heart attack, makin' me laugh so much. It not ma heart, it that buffalo, nah!"

Gina sat back on her haunches, failing to comprehend Nanderra's response. To her annoyance, Marc also roared with laughter. She wheeled around to admonish him, but Nanderra continued his explanation. "This old man is out hunting the buffalo. Makes bull buffalo angry, and he chase this old man all the way back to camp. I run like the wind, but ma wind runs away and it burn in ma chest, big mobs. I sit down until ma wind comes back. Everyone—they get excited and bring you 'ere. You good medicine for old man, make me laugh, get ma wind back." Nanderra playfully nudged Gina.

What could she say? Her relief was overwhelming. She didn't know whether to laugh or cry, but decided laughing would be more socially acceptable. Through her merriment, she mumbled to Marc,

"How on earth do I explain this one to Nhulunbuy? Can you radio Air Med and tell them it's a false alarm?"

Nanderra, still giggling, said, "Come back and visit this old man someday."

Gina seized the opportunity. "Thank you. We may come up soon and give those kids their needles to stop sickness." She had learned quickly to use any opportunity to conduct immunization clinics, especially at the outstations.

"When you come, I show you our spirit home. You good medicine." Nanderra waved goodbye as she and Marc were bustled into the wagon to return to the plane.

They headed home and talked animatedly about their day's outing. Much to Gina's relief, Air Med found the story most amusing, and so too did the resident doctor at Nhulunbuy Hospital. She was wonderfully reassuring and congratulated Gina on her initiative. It could have been serious, and based on the information to hand, you have done the right thing. "This is the Territory, Gina. We can only do our best with what we've got, and you did that. You're not to worry—this will give us all something to dine out on. Over and out."

"You must have impressed the old man," Marc observed. "To get an invitation to their spirit place is very special. Not many white fellas are so privileged."

"I am flattered. Do you know what or where their spirit place is?"

"I believe it's a huge sinkhole partly filled with artesian water near to a hidden billabong. I don't know of anyone personally who has been there. Nanderra's people believe it is the birthplace of their spirit guide. It's supposed to be like an oasis … so rumour has it."

Chapter Eight

Gina was excited about Savannah's imminent arrival. The next two weeks passed slowly but without incident. Well, almost.

Gina returned to work on a Monday morning following a quiet weekend. Mandy, her most junior health worker, had been on call. As was her usual practice, Gina checked the call-out book: *(Name) Tommy Lalarin. (Age) 8. (Diagnosis) Drowned in river. (Treatment) Panadol.*

Gina was transfixed with panic. Why hadn't Mandy contacted her? What had become of Tommy? How did one give a drowned boy Panadol?

Gina hurried towards Mandy's camp, her thoughts oscillating between disbelief and terror. Mandy came strolling towards her along the dusty road. Gina inquired, in as calm a manner as she could muster, "What happened to Tommy? Where is he? Is he all right?"

"He all right. He was playing with those kids, and they hold him under the water a little bit in the morning. Last night he got headache. I fix him, he fine this morning, nah!" came Mandy's nonchalant response.

Gina relaxed. She was slowly learning not to take things so literally and to adopt the mantra of the locals: "It's only a problem when it's a problem."

Savannah arrived from Nhulunbuy on January 5—a day Gina had anticipated with both excitement and trepidation. Even though she had written to Savannah regularly and tried to describe Lumbarta Island, she was aware that the impressions she had conveyed were tinged by her choice to work and live there. How Savannah would adapt to this lifestyle, even for a short time, Gina was unsure.

Marc was piloting the plane from Nhulunbuy and had promised Gina he would take care of Savannah. Gina had jokingly warned him to keep his distance. Life for a young man working as a remote area pilot was especially difficult given the lack of female company.

As Savannah appeared in the doorway of the plane, it struck Gina that she was viewing a young version of herself. Savannah had grown into a beautiful woman. Her honey-blonde hair was pulled back in a ponytail that displayed her natural gold-and-copper streaks. She too possessed a poise beyond her years. Her blue eyes complemented a near-perfect complexion and a trim but curvaceous body. Gina wondered where her beauty would take her. Would it influence her life choices and opportunities with the same impact Gina had experienced?

"It is so wonderful to have you here at last. I've been so looking forward to your arrival," Gina called.

"It's great to see you too, Mum."

They embraced for a prolonged time, then busily packed Savannah's belongings into the truck. Savannah excitedly related the experiences of her trip and was eager to commence her adventure in the bosom of a new culture.

The scene that unfolded as they drove into town overwhelmed Savannah to the point of silence. The many letters she had received from Gina could not have adequately described what she saw. It was obvious that it would take some time and considerable adjustment for Savannah to feel comfortable in her new environment.

Red dust covered everything. The condition of the houses was appalling. The hairless, emaciated dogs looked like something out of a space movie. People squatted outside their houses or huddled in small groups, cooking and chatting, unconcerned by a stranger's presence. Children and dogs ran among the adults creating their own chaos.

The children were the only humans who seemed aware of Savannah's arrival. They chased the truck to the health centre to get a look at "Sister Gina's girl." They looked happy and healthy, their unabashed curiosity obvious. The only other acknowledgement of her arrival was the snarling of the dogs.

Gina could almost hear Savannah's shocked thoughts. She said, "Don't let them fool you, honey child. I used to think the community didn't know or care what's going on, but believe me, they don't miss a thing. They know exactly who you are and how you fit into the picture."

Gina settled Savannah into the adjoining flat. Savannah felt quietly excited about having her own place, even if it was next door to her mother's and too small to swing a cat. It was still her very first pad.

Chapter Nine

After several days, Savannah decided to venture out into the community alone. The walls of the tiny flat seemed to be closing in on her. She wasn't sure if she could survive without creature comforts such as a television and telephone.

It wouldn't be long until Gina was finished her work shift, so Savannah left a note explaining that she'd be back by dark. The early morning and the slow-fading evening were the only times she could imagine wanting to partake in any physical exertion—it was so hot and incredibly humid. She decided to take her book and spend the last couple hours of daylight reading. She headed for the landing jetty on the river in the hope that it might be a little cooler near the water.

She wasn't far into her walk when she was joined by a rowdy contingent of community kids of various ages. They seemed fascinated by her and kept up a continual barrage of questions. "Your mudder Sister Gina, nah? Who's your farda? Where you from? Where you get that hat? Where're you going? What story you readin'? You got biscuits, nah?"

Savannah found the children's curiosity amusing and delightful. Their eager little faces mirrored enthusiasm. She enjoyed their company as she walked through town. She especially enjoyed having them along when she encountered the leather dogs, most of whom took no interest in her, although a few leapt up and snarled threateningly. For their trouble, the dogs received a whack and were yelled at, cringing back to their earthen beds under rudimentary dwellings.

The kids followed her to the jetty and sat with her for a while, wanting to know if she was going to catch some fish. She explained that she just wanted some fresh air and was going to read her book until the light faded. They continued to sit, and she felt obliged to read her book aloud. They listened with great concentration. This surprised Savannah. She would not have thought *Looking for Alibrandi* would hold their interest. She realised they probably had little experience of someone reading to them. Books would be a rarity in their homes, and many of their parents had never learned to read.

As darkness descended, the children knew it was time to go home and gradually disappeared into the fading light. Savannah closed her book and leaned back, dangling her feet over the water but not quite reaching it, trying to absorb its coolness. The river water was pristine and inviting, shimmering red and gold in the sunset. The beckoning crystal water made it hard for Savannah to accept that it was too dangerous for swimming.

Darkness descended, and the clouds covered what little moon there was. Savannah knew she should have returned before sunset. She was scared, and the darker it became, the more reluctant she was to walk back through town. She knew that, shielded by darkness, the leather dogs would be more brazen and aggressive.

"Watch out for those salty lizards."

Savannah startled and turned to see who was talking to her. It was a male voice. She couldn't see anyone. "Who's there?" she asked, trying unsuccessfully to conceal the fear in her voice and focus her eyes.

"Sorry to frighten you. I'm Balunn. Those salty lizards can easily jump high enough to take a dog from the jetty."

"Oh my God—you mean crocodiles," said Savannah, leaping to her feet and backing away from the jetty's edge.

"Yes," said Balunn, who sounded amused.

For the first time Savannah could make out the form of his body, which blended into the darkness. His white teeth were the only thing truly illuminating his position.

"Heavens, you startled me. Hi, I'm Savannah Atkins. M-my mum is the nurse here. Thank you for the w-warning," stammered Savannah.

"I know who you are." Balunn began to walk away.

She called out to him, "Balunn, do you mind if I walk back to town with you? I've been putting it off because I'm scared of the dogs—they don't like me."

Balunn slowed his pace and waited for her to catch up. "It's not you they don't like. It's your smell. They're not used to it."

Savannah felt a little indignant about being told she smelled. Balunn sensed that he'd offended her and explained. "When you came here, you probably noticed that people here smell different. I used to go to boarding school in Darwin. Most of the kids were white, and they used to tell me that I stunk. What they didn't know was that to me, their smell was offensive too. It was not a matter of washing, 'cause we all washed the same. It's just that we have a different odour, and that is why the dogs menace you."

Savannah knew exactly what he meant. She had been aware of their odour and at first found it repugnant, but soon got used to it. She appreciated his explanation.

The lights of the campfires showed the way back to town. When they reached the clinic, Savannah thanked Balunn and headed off to her flat. She noticed Balunn had been fishing and had his catch tied to a stick slung over his shoulder—two large fish, of what type she had no idea. She also noticed his fine stature.

Chapter Ten

To Aiden and Gina's surprise and misgivings, Savannah elected to stay on the island and complete her schooling by correspondence. Gina was both delighted and saddened by her decision—she was very glad of her company, but concerned for her future and the effect on her grades.

As the months passed Gina began to focus on another issue concerning children and adults on the island. The rate of immunisation among community members was particularly low. With Jalnu and the health workers, she decided to make immunisation the primary goal for the remainder of the year and into the new year. The immunisation status of everyone accessing the clinic would be checked during consultations and they would request permission to hold regular clinics at the school.

The health staff, with the assistance of the teacher Sheree, drew up a list of all children under the age of ten. They enlisted the support of the principal, Ian Turvey, and began school-based immunisation. The babies were followed up by the health workers, armed with information provided by Nhulunbuy Hospital, where most of the babies had been born.

Little birthing took place on Lumbarta Island. As was the practice in indigenous communities, women were medically evacuated during the final weeks of their pregnancies to await birth in Nhulunbuy. The women elders of the island were not happy with this arrangement. They felt that those children born in another place would remain unconnected to their land, not the way the spirits had intended.

After several meetings among the elders, Jalnu approached Gina and invited her to talk with them. The older women expressed their dissatisfaction. They cited many reasons. The accommodation provided for the women was of a poor standard. They were often harassed by drunken patrons from a nearby hotel. They had little money and no means of transport. They were without the support of the wise women of their own community at a time when it was needed most. They objected to being lumped together, designated only as "black women" with no regard for their tribal origins or language. Just because their skin was black it did not mean that they could speak with other Aboriginal women, especially those from the top end communities.

This was a perplexing problem for Gina. While she totally supported the right of the island women to birth on their own land and follow traditional practices, she knew she did not have the experience, equipment or energy to provide a safety net. It would also require her to be available to them twenty-four hours a day, seven days a week. Should a problem arise, the three hours it took to evacuate someone could mean the death of mother, baby, or both. She could not in good conscience take on this responsibility.

She offered to discuss their issues with the chief nurse, Carmen Ashdown, during her next planned visit, and invited the women to meet with Carmen, Jalnu and herself at that time. The women agreed this was a good thing and were happy with Gina's suggestion. Gina left the meeting feeling that she had let them down, but she was unable to offer any other solutions.

She was alone with her feelings. She knew these wonderful women did not share her fears about the safety of birth. They did not ask or expect her to be there for them—they merely accepted her when she was available. The fear that had been created around birth belonged to her culture and did not feature in the beliefs of this community. The women accepted birth as they did death—whatever happened was meant to be. The soul of a lost baby was simply deemed not ready for this earth but would return to another Mother in the future. Gina knew from the depths of her being that this was not a concept she could readily assimilate.

Her profound respect for these people and their approach to life deepened with each passing day.

Another problem that was worrisome for Gina erupted one quiet Saturday afternoon when she was rostered on weekend call-out. Some of the young people had taken to sniffing petrol. It involved some ingenuity on their part, as the only fuels used on the island were diesel and aviation gas—not the fuels of choice for mainland sniffers. Sadly, a few kids had managed to secure leaded petrol from the mainland.

A thirteen-year-old, Loman, had already been admitted to Nhulunbuy Hospital after a desperate call to Air Med to retrieve him. He had been brought in to the clinic by his cousin, who had found him unconscious on the outskirts of town following a seizure. Teenagers tended to gather there to share containers of fuel. They enjoyed the euphoria, ignorant of the dangers. Lead in the fuel had a cumulative damaging effect when absorbed into brain tissue, making sniffers highly susceptible to permanent brain damage.

Gina resolved to talk with Mandabartawarra about this incident and her increasing concern. Savannah shared her concern. Gina had asked her to help Yarunda look after Loman while Gina radioed for medical support. Seeing such a young boy in a seizure deeply disturbed Savannah. They were glad to wave goodbye to the Air Medical team as they lifted off to take Loman to hospital. Gina felt drained and weary. Silent tears rolled down her cheeks.

"He be all right, boss," Yarunda comforted her.

Gina wasn't so sure but was thankful for Yarunda's assistance and reassurance.

At dusk, Gina heard a knock at her flat's door. "There in a minute!"

Expecting yet another call-out, she quickly finished the remnants of her meal and answered the door. To her embarrassment, Mandabartawarra stood patiently on her veranda. She invited him in but he declined, in turn inviting her for a walk along the beach. Gina sensed that he was deeply troubled and walked with him in silence, knowing that he needed time to put his thoughts into words.

"Sister Gina," he began tentatively, "it is in my lifetime that we have come to know the white man. In 1952 the missionaries came. Before them, the Malaysians came in their boats. They fished our seas, raped our women, and took our young girls. The missionaries tried to *civilise* us—make us live the white fella way. They rounded us up and made us work on their farms and cattle stations. The missionaries brought with them other whites who gave us their diseases and their vices. They made what you call "half-caste" babies and then took them from their mothers."

"Then the new government stepped in. They say to missionaries, 'Hey, you can't do that. We have to give them black fellas back their land. Stop bossing them about. We will *save* them from you.' Then they gave us *sit-down money.*"

He bowed his head. His sadness was palpable.

"Our people, they sit down now—they don't have to work now. Their pride is gone. The young people do nothing—they sniff petrol, play cards, fight. There is no need for them to go to school. There is no need to hunt. What for? What will they do here? Why do they need to learn out of books when there's no work for them? Some do learn hunting and survival from the elders, but nothing from school that will help them here."

"We don't allow alcohol in this community 'cause it makes people crazy—they hit their wives and their children and pick fights with everyone. But now we have young people making themselves crazy from sniffing."

Gina replied carefully, "I share your concern about the sniffers. They don't seem to realise that this stuff is poison."

"Loman is my nephew. I've watched him grow from a little baby. He's a bright boy, full of life—a good boy. Now his spirit has been poisoned. He's like a headless kangaroo hopping around in circles—no sense, no direction. It makes me sad to see this happening to our children."

"How can I help? Can we ban leaded fuel? Can we vanish those people who bring it into the community?"

Mandabartawarra's face softened. "Sister Gina, you know that prohibition has never worked. We have banned leaded fuel but they bring it from the mainland. I do think maybe we can remove the kids from the petrol. We can take some of the younger sniffers away from town. They can go walkabout with the elders, hunt, practice corroboree dance, play didgeridoo, and learn bush food and bush medicine. We can prepare the boys for initiation. They're not learning from the old folks—they do not know much of the skills passed from one generation to the next."

The hurt and despair Mandabartawarra had shared with Gina was not that of a man giving up on his people but of a man truly desperate to help them. Gina felt it was not a time for her to try to solve these issues, but to feel honoured that this man of great pride and knowledge had revealed his thoughts to her. She knew those thoughts had come from a place she could never understand. Her life experiences and opportunities were very different from anything the Aboriginal people had experienced.

Gina was reminded of the reasons she had grown to hold this man in high regard.

Chapter Eleven

Savannah rose early. It was a long time since she'd been swimming, and she was looking forward to going to the waterhole. She'd decided to leave the fishing to others. Immersing herself in cool water and separating her body from the incessant heat had become an obsession. It had been very hard to resist the urge to swim in the ocean or the river. She had coveted their clarity and beauty, which she knew belied their dangers.

She was glad to be making friends. She missed her schoolmates dreadfully and was pleased to have formed a friendship with Kiah who worked with Balunn at the school. Balunn, Kiah, and Mandy had invited her to join them for a swim in the river. They were waiting on the veranda of the clinic when she arrived. Balunn had two long sticks with strings tied to them and a makeshift hook dangling on the end of each string. There were no reels or line guides. He carried nothing else—no bait, no towels, no food, no drinks. Savannah admired the way they travelled so lightly.

The group headed north out of town along a sandy track and seemed to walk forever before they reached an oasis. The waterhole was beautiful—clear emerald water flowing gently over the rocks and through two small pools before bubbling into a larger pool lined with pampas grass and paperbark trees.

Kiah and Mandy stripped down to their briefs and jumped in the water, splashing and laughing. Savannah felt embarrassed by their unabashed semi-nakedness. Thankfully Balunn kept his shorts on and seemed unfazed. He ran and leapt into the water, bombing between the two girls, causing more raucous laughter, much splashing and squeals of delight.

Savannah stripped down to her bikini and gingerly climbed down the small embankment to the water's edge to test its temperature. To her delight, it was refreshingly cool.

Before bracing herself to push off the edge, Savannah became aware that Balunn had surfaced and was drinking her in. Savannah's trim figure was accentuated by the blue-and-white bikini that complemented her blue eyes and honey-blonde hair. Although she had more clothing on than the other two girls, he made her feel as if she were totally naked. She couldn't help but feel complimented. His look was not like the many lecherous stares she had been subjected to, but rather one of open admiration.

They played and laughed and frolicked for hours before Balunn announced he was going downstream to fish. "How do you fish with no bait, fishing line or reel?" inquired Savannah.

"Come, I show you." responded Balunn.

Balunn collected his sticks, throwing his shirt across his shoulder, walked down stream. They walked along the bank a short distance, and he produced some bread from the pocket of the shirt. He kneaded it until it became doughy and pressed it onto the hook. He lowered it gently into the water and sat on the bank, inviting Savannah to sit beside him.

"What sort of fish do you expect to catch this way?"

"We'll catch a big barramundi," he assured her.

"How are you going to reel it in?"

Balunn raised his finger to his mouth. "Shh—you'll frighten them away."

Savannah got the message and sat in silence.

Suddenly Balunn sprang to his feet and scampered up the embankment as fast as he could. Sensing the danger, Savannah jumped to her feet and ran after him.

Almost instantly a large fish leapt out of the water, attached to the hook on Balunn's string. Balunn pulled the catch up. Savannah burst into laughter—she couldn't believe it. Balunn looked very pleased with himself and beamed his wonderful smile. "Here, you go," he said, rebaiting the hook and handing her the stick. "As soon as you feel a bite, take off as fast as you can."

Again they sat in silence. After two false starts, Savannah managed to hook a large barramundi. "Wow, they'll never believe this back home!" she squealed delightedly.

"Two good fish: one for you and Sister Gina, and one for my family. That's enough for today."

They walked back to the swimming hole. Kiah and Mandy were sunning themselves on a large, flat rock, hungrily devouring some bush nuts. They offered them to Savannah and Balunn. To Savannah's delight, they were tasty and filling—not unlike hazelnuts.

"We're going now. You two coming?" asked Kiah.

"I just want to have another swim to cool off after my epic dash up the embankment," replied Savannah.

"OK—we'll see you in town."

Kiah and Mandy put their clothes on and left. Savannah was a little surprised that they left without her and Balunn. Still, she realised it was not their way to influence other's actions; they simply accepted the decision.

Savannah felt a little uncomfortable alone with Balunn. She jumped into the water. Balunn followed her. "I have something to show you," he said.

Savannah almost froze on the spot, frightened that he may have misunderstood her intentions. He swam to the opposite bank and motioned for her join him. "Hold my hand, then take a deep breath," he instructed.

A little afraid not to, Savannah did as she had been told. They swam a short distance under the bank and surfaced in a dimly lit cave. Slivers of light appeared to be coming from above, refracted from the water into the cavern.

"This is the place of my family's dreaming. No other white fella has been here. It must always be our secret," confided Balunn.

Savannah looked around and couldn't believe what she saw. The roof of the cave seemed to be buttressed by huge bones. Like ribs, they were joined by a backbone that ran the full length of the ceiling. "Is this a dinosaur?" Savannah asked incredulously.

"Yes, it is. It is also the home of the serpent that protects our people. This is why you must never tell anyone. If the museum people were to find out about it, they would destroy this place."

Savannah felt honoured. "I am deeply touched that you have shared this with me. I will never mention it to anyone, not even my mum." She squeezed his arm to emphasise her promise. The power of their touch was electric. Fear again was palpable—not because of Balunn, but rather herself. "We'd best be getting back," she suggested and dove under the bank and into the sunlight.

They retrieved their fish from a small pool, where they had left them to keep cool, and headed back to town, chatting happily about school. Balunn said that he intended to remain a teacher's aide. His father was encouraging him to follow in his footsteps and become community president someday. He said he'd love to become a teacher but could not imagine leaving his community to undertake the study. He had spent too much time away at school already. Though he felt he could easily manage the academic side of university, he knew he would not have the same protection that boarding school had offered. It would be very difficult, coming from his culture and community, to embrace modern city living in the white fella's world.

Gina discussed her schooling by correspondence. She was handling it all right, but it was hard being limited to contacting her tutors by radio, and then only for a short time. She was managing most of her subjects but found maths very challenging.

Balunn smiled. "Maths—that's easy for me. I am happy to help you any day."

"Thanks. I may just have to take you up on your offer. I don't know anyone else here who has recently done year 12 maths."

Chapter Twelve

It was April 1, and Carmen Ashdown, the chief nurse, was due to visit Lumbarta Island. She usually visited every three months or so. Gina looked forward to her visits. She was grateful for the extra pair of hands that Carmen provided and for the professional updates, but also for the camaraderie Carmen brought.

Accommodation would be a little tight that night. Carmen didn't usually stay over, but she and Gina planned to work on some health issues, including birthing and petrol sniffing. Carmen would meet with the elder womenfolk during the day to discuss birthing on the homelands. She and Gina could sit down together in the evening to plan some strategies around the two issues.

Marc Bradshaw had seen Gina earlier in the week and asked if the new pilot might stay in the third health flat for a couple of nights until Wade Parker left the community. Wade had completed his term on the island. Gina had given Marc the key to the third flat. Although she was aware the new young man had arrived, their paths had not yet crossed.

Savannah had been happy for Carmen to stay in her flat for the night. Savannah would bunk in with Gina. The girl had also managed to meet the new pilot and gushed, "He is so hot, Mum. His name is Regan and he's got eyes to die for."

Gina laughed and reminded her how lonely these young men got when posted to remote places. "Those eyes may well be adorned with rose-coloured glasses, Savannah, so be wary."

The fact that Carmen would arrive on April Fool's Day had not been lost on Gina. She rallied all the health workers: Donna, Mandy, Jalnu, and Yarunda. Together they planned a right royal greeting for Carmen.

One of the things that Gina knew irked Carmen about staff working in the communities was their resistance to wearing the uniforms provided. Carmen had appealed to their sense of professionalism. She knew zippy dresses remained the usual attire, but she hoped they would pay her due respect and make an effort for her arrival.

Secretly, she conceded the wisdom of their decision not to wear a uniform, as it was so very hot in the communities. The uniforms were designed for staff working in the air-conditioned comfort of the Territory hospitals.

Wade Parker was Carmen's pilot. He touched down on the dirt airstrip with the smoothness of a feather drifting to its resting place. It was yet another clear, sunny day.

"Well done, Wade—a great day and a great flight," Carmen congratulated him.

"I'm glad you enjoyed it, but I've sad news for you. This is probably my last flight to the island. You'll have to make do without the best of the best and risk it with Marc or the new guy, Regan. I've completed my term on the island and finally got a start with Qantas. I'm stoked. I leave for Sydney in a couple of days."

Carmen laughed. "Congratulations! Marc told me he's the best of the best; is that not true?"

"No way—he's a rookie compared to me," retorted Wade.

Accustomed to travelling in small planes, Carmen easily descended the steps and waited while Wade retrieved her bag and some supplies from the front luggage compartment. She noticed Wade looking in the direction of the airstrip shed, a large smirk on his face.

Carmen turned in that direction to see all five of her health staff lined up like soldiers on parade. Their serious faces and military salutes were beguiled by the paper pan covers they had pinned to their heads, mimicking the veils of a nursing era long past. Their firearms consisted of plastic urinals and bedpans. Placards enumerating the delights of Lumbarta Island were displayed on the shed:

> *Welcome to Lumbarta Island!*
> *Home of regional shopping*
> *5-star accommodation*
> *Excellent meals—in fact you can become one*
> *A-1 health service staff*
> *Crystal-clear seas you can't swim in*
> *Heat to devour you*

"You're all ratbags," Carmen said as she greeted them with hugs, her wish for uniform compliance long forgotten along with professional formalities.

"Happy April Fool's Day!" said Gina as she cuddled her friend, boss, and mentor.

Gina and Carmen had a busy day. Gina spent the remainder of the morning in the clinic while Carmen accompanied Yarunda on his search for contacts of those diagnosed with sexually transmitted diseases. In the afternoon they met with the women elders to discuss birthing and ways to improve current practices, making them more culturally sensitive.

At the end of the day, Gina said to Carmen, "I'll lock up the clinic. You go down and freshen up, and we'll see what's in the larder for tea."

"No, no, don't bother. I've brought over a leg of lamb and some veggies. We're having a good old-fashioned baked dinner tonight. I'll get it started while you finish up. Will Savannah be joining us?"

"Yeah, I guess so—although she did mention something about a disco tonight. She's in the flat; just check with her."

Carmen knocked on Gina's door and Savannah answered. "Hi, Carmen. Do come in."

"Thanks, but I'm just checking. Your mum and I are planning a roast lamb dinner, and I trust you'll be joining us?"

"That sounds fabulous, but I told Mandy that I would go to their disco tonight. It should be interesting, and it gives me a chance to see what they do for entertainment around here and to meet some more young people. I'll give dinner a miss if you don't mind. I'm not sure what time they'll be coming to collect me. The leather dogs still frighten me, so I don't walk alone at night."

"I can understand that," Carmen said with a slight shiver, visualising the dogs she and Yarunda had encountered that day. "I'll see you later, then. Have fun."

The red dust that had accumulated throughout the day shimmied down her body as the water cleansed, refreshed, and relaxed her—the shower felt good. Carmen then busied herself preparing dinner. She put the roast in the oven and peeled the potatoes, carrots, and pumpkin in readiness for them to devour in a couple of hours. She sank into the only lounge chair in the room and picked up her novel, soon becoming engrossed in the unfolding story. She loved reading forensic fiction and had accumulated a hoard of Deaver, Reichs, and Connelly novels.

Chapter Thirteen

The evening sky was beginning to unfold its dark blanket before Carmen realised that she had not yet heard Gina return to her flat. She put the vegetables in to bake and decided to check with Savannah. Perhaps she had been so absorbed in her novel that she didn't hear Gina ascend the steps.

Savannah answered the door. "Wow, you look stunning," said Carmen. Savannah's lithe figure was scantily clad in a pink, shimmering, off-the-shoulder midriff top and a denim skirt that barely covered her butt. "Is your mum back yet?"

"No, she's still up at the clinic. When you see her, can you tell her I've gone to the disco with Mandy and Kiah? I'll see you both later."

"No problem," Carmen replied.

Carmen decided to walk back to the clinic to see what was keeping Gina—it had obviously taken longer to finish up than she'd thought. As Carmen entered the rear door of the clinic, she noticed people in the waiting area. Jalnu was fussing about in the linen room, looking for more linen.

"Jalnu, is everything OK here?"

"It fine, boss. We jus' havin' a baby is all," Jalnu calmly responded.

Hearing her voice, Gina called out, "Carmen, come on in—I need your help."

Gina quickly gave Carmen a brief summary of events. Carmen was also a midwife, and both she and Gina knew they were not "jus' havin' a baby." Jamilla was a young, first-time mother-to-be who had not had any antenatal care. Like many single women, she had managed to conceal her pregnancy from the health workers. She had arrived at the clinic as Gina was about to lock up.

Gina suspected she might be pregnant and sent for Jalnu, who questioned her and established that Jamilla was indeed pregnant. Gina thought she might have a urinary tract infection that was causing her to have premature contractions. She estimated that Jamilla was about twenty-eight weeks pregnant, or about twelve weeks early for a normal birth—this was the scary part.

Gina radioed the doctor on call in Nhulunbuy. She was relieved to hear David Peters was on duty. He outlined a treatment regime. He agreed it was an infection given the results of the urine test Gina relayed. If they could treat the infection and calm the uterine muscles with salbutamol, it might spare them all a night-time evacuation. Adding to his concern was his awareness that rain was forecast. Rain would prohibit an evacuation.

David acknowledged that they might not be successful in stopping the contractions, and urged Gina to get back to him if she thought urgent evacuation was required. Otherwise he would assess Jamilla in the morning, when he was due for a routine visit. In the interim Gina was to keep a close eye on her and radio in every hour to keep him informed.

Chapter Fourteen

Savannah waited on the clinic veranda as dusk settled in and the heat of the day began to dissipate—always a welcome respite. She looked with curiosity at her friend Kiah as she and a group of young women walked towards the building. Mandy was among them and chatted animatedly as they passed. They looked to be tarted up, and Savannah's curiosity about the disco peaked.

Kiah looked back and motioned to Savannah in her typical chin jutting, hand gesturing manner. "Hey! You comin' to the disco corroboree, nah?"

Before she could answer, Savannah noticed a group of six young men heading in the same direction. One had a boom box hoisted on his shoulder, from which techno music blared. Savannah was not partial to techno—she thought it to be mindless and repetitious.

"Thanks, Kiah, but I think I'll stay in tonight," Savannah said, suddenly feeling a little intimidated.

To her surprise, Kiah broke away from the group and walked back to her. "Boring, Savannah. You come with us. It'll be fun, nah?" She grabbed Savannah's hand and marched her off in the direction of the others.

It was dark by the time Kiah and Savannah arrived. The dance floor was a clearing in the scrub at the end of town near the beach. Everyone was up dancing. A huge fire was ignited. The roaring flames provided an epicentre of movement as they too appeared to dance to the beat. Kiah joined a mixed group of young men and women and launched her body into rhythmic movements. She motioned for

Savannah to join them, but Savannah declined, saying she'd prefer to sit and watch for a while.

The techno music took on a new dimension, and Savannah realised that it was being accompanied by the eerie and soulful sounds of a didgeridoo. She found herself readily immersed in the music of the young man skilfully harmonising this traditional instrument with the raw techno.

Savannah seated herself on a fallen tree and observed with intrigue and interest the scene before her. Before long she was aware of her body's involuntary swaying action. She was sure it was the didgeridoo that had cast its magic over her.

What struck her then was that these young people were not oppressed by the same rules as white society. They moved from group to group as they danced. Some groups were all female, some all-male, and some mixed. Their natural rhythm and their beautiful dark bodies made Savannah feel even more conspicuous. Many of these people would leave Latin American dancers for dead, she concluded. The longer she watched, the more she envied their free movement, their ability to mingle, and most of all their sheer joy and sense of fun.

She noticed Balunn silhouetted by a combination of moonlight and firelight. He was with two other young men, and they danced seductively together. This was somewhat difficult for Savannah to watch. She wondered if they were merely displaying their dance skills and considered males and females interchangeable, or whether they only fancied men. She was conscious of staring but unable to avert her gaze from this group. She had never seen anything like them. She was mesmerised by the raw sensuality of their movement and their freedom of expression.

Although the night air had cooled, Savannah felt hot. She suspected it might be more than the ambient temperature and heat from the fire that caused her discomfort.

Balunn had been watching her. When their eyes met, Savannah quickly looked away, embarrassed by her captivation. He removed his shirt and tied it around his slim hips. This only accentuated his sculptured body. Savannah couldn't help but take account of it. His broad shoulders were encased in muscle groups that seemed to be engaged in their own dance. A taut abdomen of rippled muscle fitted neatly into his narrow pelvis, which gyrated in unison. The top of his jeans just covered that which was necessary in the name of decency, closely following the lines of his firm butt and long legs.

The soft, handsome features of his face were highlighted by the most beautiful pair of big brown eyes and framed by his ebony curls. When he smiled, his face lit up like a lighthouse beacon. Savannah was captivated. The light of the fire framed the rivulets of perspiration as they ran down Balunn's chest—they too seemed to glisten to the music. Savannah was sure everyone could see that every cell of her body was erupting with excitement.

As her eyes again involuntarily traversed Balunn's body, they followed his shoulder down to an outstretched arm. To her embarrassment, his arm was directed towards her. His hand movement and eyes beckoned her to join him. She quickly averted her eyes and lowered her head, mortified that her interest was so obvious. Within seconds two brown feet appeared in the sand before her. She knew instantly that they belonged to Balunn. She looked at his outstretched hand again. Before her mind could say no, her body was on its feet, taking his hand as it folded around her own.

The moment was intense. Savannah was sure Balunn could feel her body tremble as he led her to his fireside dance place. Suddenly the whole group erupted, hooting and hollering. She looked around and realised it was for her. It certainly released the tension in her. She broke into a broad smile as she realised that no one was laughing at her; they were just showing their delight in having her join them. That was one of the qualities that so endeared these people to her: they were accepting and inclusive. Undeterred by the sight of Balunn and Savannah together, each person refocused on his or her own group.

Balunn's smile sobered as he wrapped his long arms around her petite waist. She barely reached his shoulder and had no other option than to reciprocate this move. Savannah's disdain for techno dissolved as she felt Balunn's body move to the beat. He pressed closer, gliding his hands down her back until they rested on her butt. Slowly but deliberately, he guided the movements of her body to complement his. The smell, the feel, and the movement of his body were intoxicating. Savannah knew her body was dancing, but she felt removed from it, almost as if she were drowning in a drug-induced haze—totally consumed.

To date, she had known little of the deep, instinctual feeling of lust. Now she was beginning to understand its power. Were the deep stirrings within her palpable? Did he sense that she was beyond her conscious, controlled self? Part of her wanted to run away, but the motion of the dance and the closeness of this incredible body transfixed her. Neither of them had spoken a word.

Sensual hands slowly moved over her butt. He pulled her even closer so that she felt his hardness against her. She could not free herself from this sensation, nor did she want to.

Just when she thought her insides would explode, Balunn moved his hands up the contour of her back. He caressed her shoulders, then her neck, finally curving his long fingers around her head and resting her chin in his palms. Gently he tilted her head backwards so that their eyes melded into the same pool. His full, dark lips covered her mouth, and she was engulfed—a part of him. She longed to be part of him. She explored his mouth with her tongue as his kiss lingered. Fervour took over. Their kiss changed to desperation as their bodies acknowledged the sexual tension between them.

No one else in the group seemed perturbed or interested in what was happening. When Balunn again took Savannah's hand and led her away, no one reacted in surprise. To these gentle Aboriginal people, love and making love were merely facets of life's pleasures.

They walked hand in hand along the beach. The moonlight

shimmering on the water displayed a silvery path from the water's edge to its light source. Balunn stopped, turned to Savannah, and embraced her once more. Savannah offered her lips to him, and they kissed tenderly, then with great passion. She moved her hands from his waist to his butt and grasped his firm cheeks, pulling him closer to her. They were both aware of his growing erection straining against his jeans. He slipped an arm under her thighs, lifting her feet off the ground. He lowered them both onto the sand. He drew her top over her head and caressed her virgin breasts, gently kissing her peaked nipples.

Savannah felt like she'd been hot-wired, her body tingling and hungry for him. His hand slid beneath the bottom of her skirt, and up between her legs. She was sure he felt her wetness through her briefs as he lovingly fondled her. He slipped her briefs down, and then his lips were upon her, his tongue probing every part of her. Savannah was aware of the unsolicited sounds of orgasm escaping from her soul as his long fingers and exploring tongue pleasured her senses.

She lay spent for a short time. Balunn propped himself up on his elbow and smiled. He enjoyed her look of pleasure. Savannah was happy. She felt neither judged nor compared—just special. She lay in a pool of love juice.

For the first time, Balunn spoke. "You are beautiful, Savannah. I knew this moment would be so from the first time I met you."

Savannah looked at him. She felt a little embarrassed by her self-absorption and hesitated before she spoke. "That was incredible. Um, boy, this is a little difficult." She hesitated. "I'm aware that your needs have been neglected. You were fantastic. I feel guilty that you missed out."

"My joy is being near you. My need is to pleasure you. And my orgasm came—in fact, I'll have to wash these jeans before my aunt gets hold of them. You are not yet ready for me to enter you. It will happen, but not now."

Savannah was a bit stunned, firstly by his intuition and secondly by the matter-of-fact way he spoke about the inevitability of their lovemaking. "How do you know? Why are you so sure?"

"It just is. I just know."

She decided not to pursue it. She snuggled into his body, once more drinking in the moment. She could hardly believe the events of the night and felt very lucky that her first real sexual encounter had been so wonderful. Balunn was sensitive beyond belief. She was also pleased that this experience had not been tainted by the two fears her mother constantly warned her about—pregnancy and disease.

A smile of mischief came over Savannah. "Balunn, we're lying near the water's edge—those salty lizards might get us."

"Nah. They just watching for now."

"Do you mean they really are out there?" Savannah shivered.

"Come. I'll show you."

He took her hand and helped her to stand. They walked back to the disco, asked Kiah for her torch, and returned to the water's edge. Balunn shone the torch across the water. Just beyond the definition of the moon's silvery path, they counted seven pairs of red eyes. Savannah was horrified. "We could have been *eaten*."

Balunn hugged her. "Not this time. We weren't still long enough." He added with equal mischief and authority, "They're just sizing us up for next time."

"Oh. My God," uttered Savannah.

She knew it was getting late and her mum would be concerned. "Would you mind walking me home?"

"Beautiful white fella, that will be my pleasure!" Balunn exclaimed. He bowed deeply, making Savannah giggle.

The night sky had become ominously black and now threatened rain.

Savannah arrived home to an empty flat. She concluded that Gina must have been called back to the clinic. She was glad she didn't have to answer the million and one questions her mother would ask about her evening. It would spoil her moment of indulgence and intrude upon her electrified mood.

She showered and slipped into her makeshift bed on the floor. Tired, she finally succumbed to sleep, but not before she relived every wonderful moment and re-experienced the sensation of orgasm—pure and untainted pleasure. The memory of his dark brown eyes lulled her to sleep.

Chapter Fifteen

Gina and Carmen monitored Jamilla closely. Her slight frame hardly seemed capable of birthing a baby. Her brown eyes widened with fear each time she felt a contraction. She continually sought the reassurance of Jalnu and her aunt. Jamilla's mother, Deirdra, was away at the outstation. Her extended family—two aunts and a cousin—stayed at the clinic throughout the ordeal. They too sensed the magnitude of the situation.

The contractions had settled for a couple of hours but had recommenced stronger than before. Carmen and Gina were alarmed at the prospect of such a premature infant being born on the island. Gina radioed David Peters again. "Delta, Bravo, Delta—Nhulunbuy Hospital, this is Lumbarta Island. Come in please—over."

Gina held her breath waiting for a reply. She was never too sure there would be someone on the other end.

The radio crackled into life once more. "This is Nhulunbuy. David speaking. What's happening? Go ahead, Gina—over."

"Jamilla is in labour. I have done an exam, and she is about six centimetres dilated. She seems to be progressing rapidly. I don't think it will take all that long for her to get to full dilatation. The foetal heart sounds are good. Jamilla's observations are fine. I'm concerned that the baby will be born here and there will be precious little we can do. We have some oxygen and an infant resuscitation bag and an angle-poised light that we can use to keep the baby warm, but that's it—over."

"What's the weather doing? I believe rain is forecast—over."

"It's just started to rain and is quite heavy at the moment—over."

"Shit, our plane doesn't have infant retrieval equipment and can't get into a dirt strip in the rain. I'll get onto Air Med, Darwin, and see if they can land. I'll get back to you soon. As far as the baby goes, it's probably going to be too premature to survive under the circumstances. Just do your best. I'm glad Carmen is there for moral support. I'm with you both in spirit, but there's nothing more I can do from here—over and out."

Gina sat by the radio in stunned silence, which was eventually broken by Carmen's call. "Gina, we need you!"

Gina rushed into the delivery room to find that Jamilla's water had broken. The baby's head was on view. The oxygen was attached to the infant resuscitator. The lamp was turned on to heat the wire crib—it was imperative to keep this wee baby warm if it was to have any chance of survival.

With an involuntary push from Jamilla, the tiny girl slid from her mother's loins. She cried immediately and pinked up soon after her arrival. Gina and Carmen knew this was a good sign, but also knew this gallant effort would be short-lived without their assistance. The baby's breathing soon became laboured. Carmen grabbed the resuscitator and assisted the baby to breathe while Jalnu caught the placenta, which thankfully came away spontaneously and intact.

Gina returned to the radio and put in an urgent medical call to Nhulunbuy. "Delta, Bravo, Delta—Nhulunbuy Hospital—this is an urgent medical from Lumbarta Island. Come in, please—over."

"I'm here, Gina. What's happening? Over."

"We have a baby girl born two minutes ago. She looks to be about twenty-six weeks. We are assisting her breathing with the resus bag and oxygen, and trying to keep her warm. Jamilla is fine and her placenta has been delivered safely. We request urgent evacuation—over."

"I have been on to Darwin, and they are assembling a paediatric team to retrieve baby and mother. They are concerned about the strip being wet. I need to ask—is it worth the risk of retrieval? Over."

Gina chose her words with care. "The baby appears to be in good shape. Physically she seems to be perfectly normal and is making a gallant effort to stay in this world. Yes, I think she is worth retrieving. We had a short burst of rain that rapidly subsided to a light drizzle. Over."

"It's your call. I'll get them in the air. I'll let you know the ETA as soon as advised. Over and out."

Gina rushed back to Jamilla. The girl was fine. Jalnu was monitoring her blood loss and taking observations like a veteran midwife.

"Jalnu, we'll have to radio the outstation to let Jamilla's mum know what's happening," Gina said.

Jalnu looked at Gina is disbelief and said in the most tolerant voice she could summon, "She will know."

Gina wanted to argue, but she knew this would be an insult to Jalnu. She underestimated their extrasensory perceptions and their conviction as to the reliability of information trafficked in this manner.

The tiny girl kept up her valiant efforts to breathe but required a great deal of assistance from Carmen. "I'm worried" said Carmen. "I can keep up the breathing assistance, but this lamp isn't enough to maintain her temperature. It's only 35.8 degrees and falling—any suggestions?"

Gina quickly scanned her training memories for alternative heat sources. This was not a region where one required a heater, even on the coolest days of winter. "Aha—a hot water bottle. I saw one in the spare flat. I know it's illegal in hospitals, but it's all we've got. I hope it's not perished."

She hurried out of the clinic and down the path. She ran up the staircase to the third flat. It was nearly eleven o'clock, and thankfully the light was still on. Gina rushed into the flat and past a figure sitting stark naked and totally transfixed on the bed. His look of horror, as if he had just seen an apparition, explained his lack of attempt to cover himself.

"I need the hot water bottle. It's an emergency," Gina called over her shoulder as she rummaged through the cupboard.

She was gone as quickly as she'd arrived. The stranger's presence hardly registered on her consciousness until much later, when she realised she had just met the new pilot—Regan Ayres.

Luckily the hot water bottle was intact and warmed the baby up nicely. Her tiny, translucent body remained pink and warm. David Peters had radioed back with an ETA of approximately 0145 hours—a lifetime away. Carmen and Gina took it in turns to assist the baby to breathe.

Gina's thoughts drifted to the plane. She prayed the rain would cease and allow it to land safely. The flares would guide it along the runway. "Oh my God, the flares! Jalnu, who's looking after the flares?"

"That town clerk, Karundi—it his job," replied Jalnu.

"Can you go fetch Karundi and Yarunda to put those flares out along the strip? Tell them to make sure they're fuelled up. Karundi is supposed to do that after each use."

"He s'posed to, Sister Gina, but I think him use it for his own fuel fire when there's no planes."

Gina could feel her anger rising. "Tell him Sister Gina wants those flares fuelled *now*. I don't care if he has to get his arse out of bed and open the shop or if he has to fill them himself. Tell him to get them out to that airstrip and light them. Otherwise that plane will go back to Darwin and leave this sick baby here. If you have any trouble, wake Mandabartawarra and tell him!"

Jalnu had never seen Gina lose her cool. She scurried off to relay her message.

The Air Med plane finally arrived. To the delight of everyone the rain had ceased, and the flares lighted the runway sufficiently for their pilot to land. Yarunda transported the paediatric nurse and doctor back to the clinic. After a brief introduction, they began to work on the tiny girl. Gina and Carmen could have kissed them, so relieved were they to abdicate their role.

Just prior to their arrival, Carmen and Gina had helped Jamilla cuddle her tiny infant. In so doing, Gina experienced a deeply moving moment—she too had been given this opportunity and was now able to return this life-altering gesture. Jamilla beamed a smile worth a thousand words. She tenderly kissed her daughter and with tears whispered, "Fight on, my brave girl. I love you."

Gina's tears slid down her cheeks as she relived this moment. She prayed that Jamilla's story would end more happily than her own.

After stabilising the baby and preparing her and Jamilla for the flight, Angela Green, the paediatrician, turned to Gina and Carmen. "I expected we were wasting our time coming to retrieve such a premature infant so long after her birth and in these circumstances. But thanks to you two, I hold out great hope for her chances of survival. She is in remarkably great shape."

The nurse, Scott Anderson, agreed. "You've done a great job. We'll let you know how they get on. Thank you."

Gina and Carmen could feel the tension flow from their bodies. They hadn't done too badly, all things considered.

Following the Air Med team's departure, Gina, Carmen, and Jalnu returned to the clinic to clean up. "Jalnu, you were wonderful tonight. Thank you so much. I was a little short with you earlier, but it was not you I was annoyed with. I'm sorry," said Gina.

Jalnu waved away her apology with a flip of her wrist. "No need to explain. I know that. I thank you, Sister Gina and Sister Carmen. That little baby got a good chance, nah?"

"A good chance thanks to all of us. What a team, eh?" Gina motioned to Jalnu, holding out her arms. "We need a group hug."

Gina, Jalnu, and Carmen cuddled one another and shared their tears, not knowing or caring about their origin. It could have been concern for the baby, a release of their tension, tiredness, or hunger—and was probably all those things.

Gina and Carmen said goodnight to Jalnu and headed off towards the flats together. The odour of over-roasted lamb wafted to their nostrils simultaneously, and they began to laugh. Carmen motioned towards her flat. "Madam, can I interest you in our char-roasted lamb with miniature shrivelled vegetables on the side?"

"Hell, you can! I could eat the proverbial fork out of a nightie right now."

They cleaned up, set the table, and sat down to eat perhaps the driest but also the tastiest roast dinner they had ever had. They devoured it, suddenly conscious of an insatiable hunger that overrode their extreme tiredness.

After a cursory clean-up, they bid each other goodnight. "I think a sleep-in is in order for the morning," said Carmen, herself exhausted.

"If only I could. The hot sun wakes me early. Goodnight, Carmen. I'm sure glad you visited—thanks so much for your help."

"Don't thank me. I was glad to be able to help, but I'm equally sure you would have coped without me."

Chapter Sixteen

Carmen flew back to Nhulunbuy the following day. She was aware that Gina's exhaustion was tinged with sadness—not just for Carmen's departure, but something more. Perhaps the constant demands of working in the communities? In any case, Gina had found the whole experience particularly difficult, and that was more than likely personal and not professional. "We'll get you into town next week, Gina. You need a break. I'll organise some in-service training for you and a locum—that way I can legitimise the expense."

Gina too was aware of her tiredness as she waved the plane off. Tears welled in her eyes. She was grateful for Carmen's intuitive and diplomatic acknowledgement of her demeanour.

David Peters had arrived on the same plane that Carmen boarded. As Gina drove him to town, she was aware of a feeling of dread. She was just too tired for doctor's clinic. David seemed to sense this. Gina thought Carmen might have prompted his empathy as they exchanged words on the airstrip. "Go have a rest, Gina. The health workers and I ran the clinics alone before you arrived. One day more won't matter," he said with a friendly caress of her shoulder.

Damn it, Gina thought as the tears began to flow freely. *That's all I need—a bit of sympathy and I'm a mess.* "I'll be OK, thanks. I'm just a bit tired," she said aloud. She had some issues she needed to discuss with him, and felt compelled to make the best of his short visit.

Gina was preparing for the clinic when she heard the radio crackle into life. "Alfa, Foxtrot, Delta—three six eight. Calling Lumbarta Island clinic. Over."

Jalnu answered, "Lumbarta clinic here—over."

"Lumbarta, this is Joel Andrews speaking, skipper of the *Lady Pristine*. I run one of the prawn trawlers in the gulf. I've just picked up a bloke floating in the straits, over."

"Joel Andrews, this is Jalnu, head health worker at the clinic. We had a big night last night, and I'm in no mood for nonsense. Nothin' we can do for dead'uns. Over."

"I'm not joking. We picked him up about half an hour from the island. He is very much alive. Can you organise to fly him out?"

Gina was now standing beside Jalnu, and Jalnu handed her the radio. "Mr Andrews, this is Gina Atkins, clinic nurse at Lumbarta Island. Can you tell me the condition of the man and elaborate on the circumstances? Did he fall overboard? Over."

"Hi, Gina. He's not in too bad shape. A bit waterlogged and shivering, but coherent. Apart from being sunburnt, he looks OK. No, he didn't fall overboard. He says he just went for a swim. I'll explain when we arrive. Over."

Gina inquired further, "Hell of a spot for a swim. If he's not too bad, I'd like to bring him here. We have a doctor visiting today. I'd like to get him checked over before we call Air Med. Can you come into the island landing? We'll have transport waiting when you arrive. Over."

"No problem. We're on our way. ETA approximately 1330 hours. Over and out."

The doctor's clinic would have to wait today. Gina collected some monitoring equipment, blankets and water. She relayed the story to David, who saw a couple of clients before they headed to the landing to meet the swimmer. "I can't believe anyone would go swimming in these waters," said Gina in exasperation.

"Yes, it is rather hard to believe, especially in light of another incident we had last month at Nhulunbuy."

"What happened?"

David explained, "A visiting electrician had one too many and announced he was going to swim out to his yacht moored in the bay. All the locals warned him about the crocs and told him to stay put. The bay's notorious for crocs—it's their breeding ground. Well, this guy decided he was going anyway, and that was the last his mates saw of him."

"Oh my goodness!" Gina exclaimed. "Do they know what happened to him?"

"Well, yes, actually, we know exactly what happened to him. I was called out the next day to the shores of the bay. They'd caught a big croc with an overfull belly. They cut him open and hauled out body parts—a head, part of a torso, and an arm. The croc probably stashed the rest, as they prefer their food putrefied."

"Oh dear, how awful. That must have been very distressing for you and especially his family—having to identify the bits." Gina grimaced at the thought of the grisly find.

"Yeah, it was pretty upsetting. But you know, those Timex watches work well. It hadn't missed a beat. Ticked away merrily on the arm as if it were on a mannequin in a shop window."

Gina and David laughed—not at the poor fellow's misfortune, but in acknowledgement that sharing black humour enabled health personnel to bear the unbearable.

They pulled up at the landing wharf just as the trawler docked. David, Gina, and Yarunda jumped out of the truck and waited for the vessel to be secured. David and Yarunda climbed aboard, turning to help Gina. They were invited inside the cabin. A man was sitting up at the galley table, his legs extended before him. He was a scruffy-looking character with ginger beard and ginger hair. His sunburnt skin that was not dissimilar to that of the leather dogs.

Gina introduced them all and set about taking some observations while David asked for his story. "Name's Blue—alias Fred Dawson," the man said as he extended his gnarled hand to David. "It's like this, Doc. Me and the boys got on the piss last night. We were camped on the north of the island. The boys must have slept it off on the beach.

I remember thinking I'd rather get back to my bed on the boat. I decided to wade into the water and head for our boat, the *Northern Star*. I dunno what happened then. I must have blacked out.

"The next thing I remember was waking up. I felt all around me, and all I could feel was wetness. I thought, 'Oh, shit, I've pissed the bed.' Then I opened one eye, all the time feeling like I was floatin', and bugger me dead, I was. All I could see was the sea."

David listened intently. "So where were you exactly?"

"I don't exactly know. The current musta picked me up. I ended up about five nautical miles north of the island. I realised I was in big trouble. I could see another small island in the distance and thought I'd be better off staying with the sharks and stingers. At least they're well fed in these waters. If I swam for the island, I'd never be seen by passing boats, and I'd have to take my chances with the crocs.

"So I just kept on floatin'. That's when I saw the *Lady Pristine*, like a mirage. I thought she was gonna miss me at first, but thank Christ she turned in my direction, and Joel and his boys here picked me up. And here I am. I think I'll join the priesthood when I get back to civilisation—don't ya reckon, Doc?"

"I can't believe this," Gina said. "If it weren't for those deep crevasses in your hands and feet and your low body temperature … All I can say is that someone must be looking after you, Fred Dawson."

"For sure," agreed David. "You seem to be in remarkably good shape for a bloke who's spent the night in the ocean. You're lucky the gulf waters are warm. I don't think we need to fly you out. Just take it easy for a few days. Sister Gina will put some burns cream on you and get you warmed up. She will keep an eye on you overnight. You can leave with Mr Andrews in the morning—if that's OK with him. You need to report to your doctor or the hospital as soon as you're back on the mainland."

After they returned to the clinic and settled Blue, Gina left instructions for his care with Yarunda. Then she took David to the airstrip for his return flight to Nhulunbuy. She was glad to finally return to her flat.

She called in to see Savannah on the way and was surprised to find her on the veranda. Books were strewn all over a low occasional table, and Gina's favourite lamp lit the work. Savannah was seated on a cushion on the floor. Next to her sat Balunn.

"Oh, hi, Mum," Savannah greeted her. "Balunn is a whiz at maths. He's helping me with trigonometry."

Balunn stood politely. "Hello, Sister Gina. I hope you don't mind."

"Not at all. I'm delighted that Savannah has found someone who is able to assist her. Maths is not her strong subject and certainly not mine. I'm going to turn in now, Savannah—I'm beat. It's been a long couple of days. I'll see you in the morning. Will you be all right to get yourselves something to eat?"

"Sure, Mum. I know you had a big one last night. Sleep well."

"Yes, we did, and that has been followed by an eventful day. I'll tell you about that in the morning. Not too late, you two. Goodnight to you both."

As Gina turned to leave, she saw something resembling a look of allegiance flash between Balunn and Savannah. It made her feel uneasy, but she was too tired to concern herself.

It wasn't until the following week, when she was preparing to leave for Nhulunbuy, that Gina's concern returned. She had been surprised that Savannah was happy for her to go alone. Savannah was usually very keen to leave the island, especially when given the opportunity to reacquaint herself with her favourite pastime—shopping.

Gina ventured, "You know, these people's culture is far removed from ours. It would only end in heartbreak for you both if you were to get too close to someone here. You come from different worlds, and neither can fully appreciate that of the other."

"What are you talking about, Mum? Are you saying these people are good enough to live with, work with, and become friends with, but not good enough to love?"

"No. These people are just as good as you and me and every other race. But your life paths and experiences are so divergent—I just don't want you to get hurt. I sense that you like this boy. Am I mistaken?"

"Not entirely. But I just don't see the problem. He is caring, kind, gentle, and very understanding—more than you'll ever know, and more than anyone else I have ever met."

"Savannah, my love, I'm sure he is. Balunn is a fine young man who will someday make a fine president like his father. But ultimately he will stay here and you will move on. He wouldn't survive in your world nor you in his. You're so young and have your life ahead of you. There are many more young men to meet. Please be careful, for both your sakes. I love you and don't want to see you get involved in something way over your head that can only end in pain."

Gina hugged her daughter as she left but still felt very uneasy as she boarded the plane.

Chapter Seventeen

The following day, Savannah settled into what she called her "comfy cush." She had carted her multi-coloured bean bag from one end of the nation to the other. She always reflected upon their winter days in Melbourne whenever she used it.

She began to watch her favourite movie, *Ten Things I Hate About You*. Heath Ledger was the man. She had fantasised over interludes with him more than once.

She and Balunn had arranged to go over some more maths problems later that day. She was aware of her anticipatory excitement and tried to dull it by concentrating on the movie.

Balunn knocked on the door at five o'clock as arranged. Unlike many of his people, he had a passion for punctuality. *Probably a combination of boarding school training and his teacher's aide work,* thought Savannah. "Come in! Thanks for coming over. Are you going to stay for tea? I've made up some tuna mornay if you're interested."

"I feel I should say no, but I can't resist an invitation from you." He smiled.

They sat out on the veranda, again cross-legged on the floor, and began to work through Savannah's latest maths assignment. They worked well together and chatted on a superficial level, but there was an unspoken magnetism between them.

Each night that Gina had been away, Balunn had come over. They'd worked together under the light of Gina's favourite lamp until about nine thirty, when Balunn would excuse himself politely and leave. It was driving Savannah crazy. She wanted him so much, she ached all over. She told herself that he obviously had regrets about the night of the dance, and this made her feel sad and unwanted.

This was the night before Gina was due to come home. Savannah could stand it no longer. "I feel there are some things we need to talk about," she ventured. "There's some stuff between us that I don't understand. I'm feeling that you're sorry about our night on the beach."

Balunn stopped. His shoulders dropped, and he looked at her with a questioning tilt of his head. "Savannah, our worlds are so different. You will soon leave to go on your half-year break to Melbourne. You will return to your friends and your life. It will be hard for you to come back here once you've been reminded of what you're missing. At the end of the year, you will leave here forever. I won't see you again. You will follow your dreams and go to university and study sociology. This life will be long forgotten."

He paused, deep in thought. "I have a duty to our people. My father wants me to take over as president someday, and I have much to learn."

A cloud descended over Savannah. She sensed the truth in what he was saying. The truth hurt. "Surely you will be able to offer your people more if you come with me to uni? You're super smart. You could be a teacher, not just an aide."

That familiar broad smile crept over Balunn's face. "You are smart too. But I believe my people expect me to stay here and learn their ways, not the ways of the white fella world."

"Surely you would be able to negotiate so much more for your people if you observe the way white fellas play the game of life."

"That's a good point, but one that would be lost on many of my people. They have had little to do with the white fella ways. They expect me to stay here."

Savannah went quiet. She was feeling exasperated when Balunn rose to leave. She sensed that she had offended him. They walked to the door.

Without warning, Balunn embraced her fervently. His arms wrapped around her and lifted her in one manoeuvre. He leaned back against the wall of the entry. He kissed her deeply and desperately as her legs folded around him. He nuzzled into her neck. "Savannah, never, as long as I have breath in my body will I be sorry about any second I have spent with you. You are beautiful beyond words. I love you beyond the sky. I want to make love to you for all the sunrises of my life—but I know this can't be. When I leave you, I can't sleep. I can't eat. You are in my mind when my mind should be filled with other things. I carry around a big stone in my belly that twists and turns a thousand times a day. I know you want me inside you, and I want that more than you will ever know. But I am afraid this will drive a spear through my heart and yours. That is why I leave. It takes all my will, but I must do this."

He gently lowered her legs until they took her weight. He placed a kiss on her forehead, each of her eyes, her cheeks, and lastly her mouth. Then he turned and ran down the steps, out of sight.

Tears rolled down Savannah's face as she stood forlorn in the doorway. She sobbed and smiled at the same time. She was angry and frustrated. She wanted him to make love to her. Her whole body tensed at the thought of their being together. She was also in awe of him, his strength, and his insight. Balunn was not someone she could stay mad at. She knew what he had said was true.

Chapter Eighteen

The week in Nhulunbuy was just what the doctor ordered. The R & R made Gina feel like a new woman. She shopped, dined out, visited former colleagues, and caught up on the regional gossip. She bought food, books, and clothes—mostly for Savannah, who looked great in just about everything.

She and Carmen also went hunting for crabs and mussels in the mudflats with Rosemary and Margery, two of the Aboriginal health workers from Yirrkala, an Aboriginal settlement on the outskirts of Nhulunbuy. Gina was terrified that her toes would be missing at the end of their trek but was reassured by these two women, who seemed very comfortable traipsing bare-footed through the mangroves in mud up to their calves. Gina at least had on a pair of very muddied sneakers that provided a false sense of protection from the powerful claws of the crabs.

Rosemary and Margery moved with great stealth. Gina and Carmen bore the brunt of their mirth as the white women tripped over every mangrove root. The mud seemed to engulf them as they tried to follow in the footsteps of their expert teachers. It was fun though, and Gina loved being able to get down and dirty for the first time since her childhood.

As she approached the Nhulunbuy airport on her way back to Lumbarta Island, she wondered if the other "best of the best" might be flying today. She enjoyed Marc's company, and it had been a while since she last saw him. To her minor disappointment, it was not Marc but another young man she barely remembered.

"Regan Ayres, pilot extraordinaire. And I must say you are looking a little less preoccupied than when we first met."

Gina shook her head, bemused by the brimming confidence of youth and laughed. "Yes, I do remember, Regan. I'm sorry if I was rude. It was a tough night."

"Well, if you were as rude as I was nude, we can cancel out the need for an apology."

Another thing Gina remembered was Savannah's summation of this young man—he was indeed hot. His eyes were like blue-green pools of crystal. He stood about 165 centimetres tall, and his brown locks fell comfortably around his beautifully etched face. He also had a great butt and tanned, well-shaped legs—a feature Gina never missed in a man.

"Well, young Regan, take me home. I've had a great week, but it's time to go back to my daughter and the community." Gina climbed the aircraft steps.

"It seems there's only the two of us, so if you want to ride up front, you're welcome," he offered.

"OK. That would be great. Thanks, Regan."

Gina had certainly become a lot more comfortable with small plane travel. She now thought nothing of the flight—it was just a means of transport. One day she might even learn from her indigenous friends how to travel with few possessions—but not today. She had two additional bags to take home on top of the one she had arrived with.

Gina buckled up and settled in for a relaxing trip. The skies were blue and the winds light. She admired the take-off, which was as smooth as any she had experienced to date. They soon levelled out over the blue gulf.

The distant silhouette of Lumbarta Island came into view. Gina sat forward in an alert position and sniffed the air. "I can smell smoke," she said with concern.

"I don't think so. But just in case—can you swim?" Regan said, making light of it. Gina could see that his brave face was hiding the fact that he too could smell it.

In the next few seconds, the cockpit began to fill with smoke. Gina was terrified. She looked out the window to see how far away the island was and to size up her chances if the plane were to ditch into the ocean. She prayed and looked at Regan, appealing for reassurance that this was normal, nothing to worry about. She could see by the look on his face that he couldn't give her that reassurance.

He urgently radioed air traffic control. "Bravo, Foxtrot, Alpha— Mayday, Mayday. This is Regan Ayres from North East Airlines, flight two, three, eight out of Nhulunbuy. I have a fire on board. One passenger, Gina Atkins, headed for Lumbarta Island. About five nautical miles from airstrip—will try to land. Over."

"Oh shit, Regan. shit, shit, shit" was all she could say.

"We'll be all right. We're too young to die."

"I'm a bloody lot older than you, and I don't think age comes into it," Gina retorted.

"I'm scared too. I'm sorry. This is not the usual level of comfort I like my passengers to experience."

The cockpit had filled to the point where it was difficult to breathe or to visualise the horizon. Gina held on tightly to Regan's leg as he worked hard to steady the plane and keep in control. "We're nearly there," he gasped. "I'm going to try something. It's worked before. Hang on tight."

With that he put the plane into a sudden steep dive. Gina felt her insides slam to the back of the plane. She closed her eyes and hung on for all she was worth.

Remarkably, the smoke cleared. The plane hobbled towards the airstrip.

"Now, Gina, as soon as I land, I want you to open the window, OK?"

Gina nodded, unable to say a word.

"Then when the plane stops, I want you to climb out the window, jump to the ground, and run as fast as you can—got that?"

"Jump down and run," Gina mumbled. "Got it." She closed her eyes again and waited to feel the tyres crunch into the ground.

At the first bump, Gina undid the latch and flung the window open. Regan slammed on the brakes, sending the plane skidding across the gravel strip. It spun to a halt. Gina shimmied through the window, jumped to the ground, and ran as fast as she could past the fuel shed and out to the edge of the road. She was too scared to look back.

When she finally stopped running, she sat down heavily on the ground and looked towards the plane. The motors were shutting down, but still there was no sign of Regan. Should she go back to see if he needed help? No, she had been told to run.

From the other side of the plane, Regan finally appeared. He was running at full pace towards her. When he reached her resting place, he too sat down heavily beside her. They watched the plane and waited in silence, both knowing what they were waiting for—the explosion.

It never happened. They eventually realised that the fire had gone out. Gina relaxed and let her emotions flow. She leaned on Regan's shoulder. "I declare you better than the best of the best. I'm impressed. I've never been so bloody scared in all my life," she said as her body insisted on maintaining its tremble.

"Not a bad piece of flying, even if I do say so myself," Regan said admiringly.

They sat for a while longer. Gina said, "You said it had worked before. Do you mean to say you've had this happen more than once?"

Regan put his arm around her in comfort. "Well, not exactly. I read it in a Biggles book when I was about ten. Biggle's fuel line caught on fire, and he extinguished it by putting the plane into a steep dive. I had no other tricks, so I thought it was worth a try."

Gina looked at him in disbelief. "I'm so glad you didn't share that with me up there. I think you just saved my life, but I don't want to know any more about how." She didn't know whether to laugh or cry. She felt relieved and very grateful.

Chapter Nineteen

Gina was sure glad to see Savannah. She related the events of her trip home. Savannah was shocked. To think her mother could have died … That was a little too close for comfort.

They shared a lot of time together before Savannah's departure to Melbourne for the mid-year holidays. It was winter—if you could call it that. The days were warm but the evenings and nights were cool. Savannah had seen little of Balunn. When their paths crossed, their greetings were cordial but reserved. She knew it was as difficult for him as for it was for her.

Savannah and Gina spent a great deal of time walking the beach and collecting shells. They talked about anything and everything. They talked about Balunn. "It's probably for the best, Savannah. Balunn is right. A relationship between you would have to end in sadness. Although I understand that it is very hard to overrule your heart. In the best interests of all concerned, this is what has to be done. I admire you both for being sensible."

"I hate being sensible," sighed Savannah. "I miss him heaps."

On the morning of her return to Melbourne, Savannah awoke early. She showered and attired herself in a lightweight blue top and jeans. For the first time in many months, she put on closed-toe shoes and some socks. She packed her blue denim jacket and woollen coat in the outside pocket of her bag so she could easily retrieve them in Darwin before checking her bags forward to Melbourne. Her coat smelled of camphor. The flakes she had put with it to protect it from silverfish fell, like snowflakes, to the ground. This reminded her of how cold it would be in Melbourne mid-year. She wasn't looking forward to the cold weather. But her excitement about seeing her friends and Aiden overshadowed her concerns. She missed them all. She would also miss Balunn and felt melancholy about the fact that the distance between them had grown.

Gina was waiting at the truck. She had the rear doors open, ready for Savannah to load her luggage. The closer Savannah came to departure the heavier her bags seemed to be. She heaved them into the back, conscious that she was surreptitiously searching for signs of Balunn. He knew she was leaving today—she had hoped he might say goodbye. She slumped into the front seat, knowing that it probably was not his way, to say farewell.

Marc was flying today and had already completed the pre-flight check of the aircraft when Gina and Savannah arrived. There were no other passengers, just some cargo to load. "All aboard," called Marc.

Gina and Savannah embraced. They both felt a little teary for their own reasons, and hated saying goodbye.

Gina stood well clear of the aircraft. The engines surged to life, propelling dust in all directions. They taxied out to the end of the airstrip, and the motors roared at Marc's command. As the revs increased, the aircraft moved down the runway, gathering speed.

Savannah glanced out the small window. There on the far edge of the airstrip stood Balunn. His long body was straight and proud as he stood on his left leg, right foot resting comfortably on his left calf. His spear leaned lightly against his shoulder. He lifted his arm, more in a salute than a wave. Savannah glimpsed his body sliding to a sitting position as the aircraft lifted off, his image becoming obscured in its dusty trail.

Her melancholy overcame her, and her tears flowed.

Landing in Melbourne raised her mood as she anticipated her father's welcome. She had written often to Aiden and knew that he too was looking forward to their reunion.

As she entered the airport lounge, she saw Aiden. He looked great, somehow healthier and definitely somewhat slimmer. She flung her arms around him and they embraced for some moments. He stood back from her, holding her at arm's length. "Let me look at you," he said admiringly. "My goodness, what have you done with my little girl? She's transformed into a beautiful young woman! Don't tell me I have to spend the next two weeks chasing away those misfits of boys you went to school with."

Savannah giggled and hugged him again. "Stop it, Dad—you know I've only come to see you."

"Oh, yeah. I'm flattered. I'll give it a day or two, and you'll be off seeking the company of your friends—as I'd expect."

"As you would."

They each put an arm around the other and headed for the baggage claim.

That evening, Alexa came to dinner. She greeted Savannah with greater than usual gusto and squeezed her so hard Savannah thought she'd burst. "How's it going, kid? Bugger me, I take that back. You're no kid anymore. Something's changed, and I'm not sure that it's just that you're prettier and more womanly than when you left."

They moved into the lounge. While Aiden prepared a drink for each of them, Alexa launched into a tirade of questions. "How's your mum? She ready to come home yet? I've had a promotion—now the national editor, you know. I need good people like her. Tell her when she's finished playing nurse to get her arse back down here. I'll be waiting. And what of you, young lady? Caught yourself one of those hunky young pilots yet?"

Savannah laughed. "No … too busy studying."

"What? Bullshit. You forget, I was your age once!" Alexa exclaimed with a laugh. "Nobody studies that hard. If you are, then it's time you and I had a big talk about the three most important things in life: sex, sex, and more sex."

"It's good to see you haven't changed," said Savannah, slightly embarrassed.

"What?" interjected Aiden. "You've been here two minutes, and already you're trying to corrupt my innocent daughter?" He handed around the drinks.

"Innocent, my arse. Are all fathers blind, or do they just choose to pretend they are? Maybe they're plain stupid. I'm constantly amazed at what men forget from the time they're young dogs to when their daughters reach the same age … or younger! So if it's not a young pilot, who is it? Must be someone that's put that cherry in your cheek. Who the hell else is there?"

Much to her annoyance, Savannah could feel her cheeks colouring as a wave of heat rose from her neck to her face.

"Aha—so there are other options. You can tell me later when that ostrich of an old man of yours is not around," Alexa whispered conspiratorially.

Chapter Twenty

Following Savannah's departure, Gina began planning the immunization clinics that would be held when school recommenced. She arranged with the school principal, Ian Turvey, to conduct clinics over two weeks. With the aid of the health workers, each child's records had been checked. The health workers were invaluable in assisting Gina to sort out who was who, where they lived, and who to speak with to obtain consent to have the children immunized. This was not always the mother or father of the child. In many cases, the aunts and grandmas had more say than the parents.

She also planned to visit Nanderra's people at the Curraba outstation. She radioed the outstation. Nanderra was happy to have Gina and Jalnu visit to conduct a clinic. Savannah was not due to return until mid-February. *The more you pay, the less time at school,* Gina surmised.

Gina confirmed the visit with Nanderra. "I kill a buffalo and we have a feast," he joked over the radio.

"No, thank you, Nanderra. It's my turn to supply the tucker. I don't want you chasing any more buffalos," chided Gina.

She also reminded him, "Last time you mentioned your sacred place in the rocks. I wonder if you would mind if we camped there for the night—after our feast of course. Please say if it's not OK for me to ask."

"It OK, but I think Jalnu can't go. It's not her dreaming place. She stay with us. You go."

"Is it the big sinkhole?"

"No," replied Nanderra. "That Goobunji land-belong my brother's people. I will show you."

"Thanks. Maybe I can talk the pilot into coming with me—to chase away those buffalos!" Gina laughed. "Would that be OK?"

"OK."

Marc Bradshaw called in to the clinic that evening to radio his family via Darwin. Gina approached him about flying Jalnu and her to the outstation. "No probs. I'd love to. How long will the clinic take, and when do you want to go?"

"I've planned it for next Friday if you and your plane are available. The clinic itself should take at least four hours. I'll do a full check on the kids because they don't get into town very much."

"Um, Friday … We may have to camp overnight and come back Saturday."

"I was planning to anyway. I've promised Nanderra a feast in the evening. I'm really excited 'cause he's given us permission to camp at the sacred rocks. I'd love to explore them. It's a privilege that not many white fellas will know."

"Fair dinkum," replied Marc, equally enthusiastic. "I've only heard about that place—I'd love to see it. Great work!"

The school immunization clinics went well. Gina, Mandy, and Donna set up a production line—Donna checking names and records, Mandy drawing up the injections and giving the oral Sabin, and Gina completing the task by giving the injections. Balunn was a great help. He kept the kids entertained while they waited, which helped reduce their anxiety. And he consoled them with a hug when needed. Yarunda and Jalnu stayed at the health centre and conducted business there as usual.

By Wednesday they had completed the immunizations and checked the hearing, skin, eyesight, and posture of all the children at the school.

Gina had ordered sufficient vaccine and medical supplies for the visit to Nanderra's outstation. Arranging extra food was delegated to Marc. He was flying to Darwin on Tuesday. Gina was grateful to have him shop for the feast—getting fresh supplies for the twenty or so people who lived at the outstation was not easy. They were fortunate to have a plentiful supply of bush tucker and fish. Marc would leave Nhulunbuy on Thursday morning, returning to the island by mid-afternoon.

On Thursday, while Gina, Jalnu, Mandy, Donna, and Yarunda were taking a well-earned break following a very busy morning, they heard Marc's plane overhead, right on schedule. He circled the health centre to let them know he'd arrived. Gina despatched Yarunda to the airstrip to collect the food for their outstation visit. Few supplies could be transported on the old 250 cc Honda bike Marc used to go to and from the airstrip.

It was some time later that Gina heard Yarunda return. She wondered what had taken so long. Laden with groceries, he despondently pushed the clinic door open. Gina looked up from the health charts. "What's wrong, Yarunda?" she inquired as they placed the food in the fridge.

"That fella—he trouble, that one."

"What fella?"

"That Ebaneza—he a bad man, full of booze. He come back 'ere with Marc."

No sooner had Yarunda finished speaking than Gina heard what she thought sounded like firecrackers.

Yarunda bolted outside to see what was going on. People were yelling and scurrying in all directions. Gina followed Yarunda outside and caught a glimpse of someone lying on the ground. A man with a gun was heading towards them.

"Back inside, quick!" yelled Yarunda.

He followed Gina in and locked the health centre doors. He called to the other health workers to get down. Gina was frightened, more by Yarunda's reaction than by the actual event. Then she heard shots close by and realised the man was shooting indiscriminately. Some of his bullets were finding the clinic walls. She crawled as quickly as she could to the radio in the adjoining room. "Victor, Bravo, Foxtrot, one niner eight!" she shouted.

"Air Med emergency channel. What is it? Over."

"God, Nancy, am I glad to hear you. We're under siege here. There's a bloke running around with a skin full of booze and a gun, and he's shot someone. I can't get out to see if the person is alive. We've locked all the doors. He's shooting at the clinic. Yarunda says he's drunk, that he just got off the plane from Darwin. Over."

"Stay put. I'll contact Nhulunbuy police. Stand by. Over."

After what seemed an interminable time, Nancy's voice interrupted the tension. "Gina, Nhulunbuy police are on their way, ETA approximately one hour. Stay where you are and don't attempt to apprehend this fellow. Keep your head down. I'll be here if you need me. Over and out."

Gina, Mandy, and Donna lay still and waited. Jalnu and Yarunda had crept towards the back of the clinic, whispering to one another as they went.

"Don't do anything silly you two," Gina hissed. "Wait for the police. They'll be here soon."

Yarunda called back in a hushed voice, "I go and get my spears. I spear him. He can't just shoot up our clinic."

"No, no, Yarunda, you can't spear him. You'll end up in jail instead of Ebaneza!"

Before Gina could say any more, the back door of the clinic opened and Yarunda was gone. Jalnu locked it after him. "Jalnu, what are you doing?" Gina demanded.

"Yarunda's getting help. They stop that man."

Gina knew there was nothing more she could do. This was their way. They dealt with things their own way and punished wrongs by their own unwritten laws.

Quiet descended, except for the beating of Gina's heart, which she felt could be heard above a rock concert. Suddenly there were sounds of a scuffle. Gina slowly raised her head to look out the window. She saw Yarunda, Balunn, and two other men standing over the assailant. Balunn was tying his hands behind his back. Yarunda had a foot on the captive, like a great black hunter savouring his trophy.

"Victor, Bravo, Foxtrot, one niner eight—you there, Nancy? Over," Gina radioed.

"Yes, I'm here. Are you OK? How's it going? Over."

"The guys have captured the shooter. I'm going to see how the victim is. I'll get back to you. Over."

Gina grabbed her first aid kit and headed off with Jalnu following.

The identity of the victim quickly became evident. It was Karundi, the town clerk. *He probably needed shooting*, thought Gina as she attended to him. Karundi was a shady character who had been highly protective of the financial aspects of council business when she and Mandabartawarra had questioned the council's ability to pay for breakfast at the school. Gina couldn't help but feel he was fearful some form of impropriety would be exposed.

Karundi was curled up in a ball trying to protect himself. He was bleeding through his shirt. He spoke to Gina and explained what had happened. Gina summoned help to take him to the clinic, where she examined him more closely. Fortunately for Karundi, Ebaneza had used a shotgun with duck shot pellets. The pellets had sprayed all over Karundi's chest and lodged superficially in his chest wall. Gina radioed Air Med to let them know the extent of Karundi's injuries and the need for his evacuation.

As Gina was writing up her notes, Yarunda came rushing into the clinic. "Where that Marc? He in big trouble."

"What do you mean? What's he done?" asked Gina.

"He bring that Ebaneza 'ere. 'Cause him shoot up the town clerk, some fellas looking for 'im. He gotta get out of town quick," urged Yarunda.

"Look after Karundi," instructed Gina as she hurried out of the clinic towards Marc's flat. She didn't understand this aspect of blame but had learned not to question it. Marc's safety was at risk. Gina ran up the few stairs to the flat that Marc and Regan shared and rushed in unannounced. "Marc—grab your things, get on your bike, and get out of here quickly. They're blaming you for Karundi's shooting," Gina blurted out.

Marc was bewildered. "They're what? How in the hell can they blame me? He had a can of Coke, or so I thought. I had no idea it was full of rum till well into the flight, when he started to play up. What was I supposed to do, turf him out into the ocean?"

"I don't know. All I can say is don't try and reason just now. Get in your plane and get out of here. It may blow over in a day or two, but for now, just leave."

Marc did as Gina suggested. He threw his clothes and toiletries in a bag, jumped on his bike, and motored out of town as quickly as he could.

Regan came over to Gina, stunned by the unfolding events. "How can they blame him? These people are hard to fathom. Sometimes you think you know them, then something like this happens and you realise you don't. They'll replace Marc—the company would never risk him returning here."

"I'll miss him," replied Gina. "He was a friend. Oh … bugger. I'd arranged an outstation visit tomorrow. Marc was going to fly Jalnu and me up to Nanderra's camp to do a clinic."

"I can take you," offered Regan. His fuel line had been replaced. Gina could see he was thankful to have an excuse to escape the tension in the community.

"You haven't flown up that way, have you?"

"I've flown over many times."

"It's just that the strip up there is fairly short and rough. It's not even a real strip; it's nothing more than a broadened stretch of dirt track."

Regan spread his arms out, palms facing upwards, in mock seriousness. "Come on, Gina! Didn't this man just save your life? Now you're questioning his flying skills!"

Gina smiled. "You're right. I know you're better than the best of the best. It's just that we were going to camp up there for the night. I promised Nanderra a feast, and in exchange he was going to let Marc and me camp and explore the sacred rocks. That's their dreaming place."

"I know—Marc told me. I'd love to see it if you'll take me. I know he bought a heap of food. I'll grab it."

The following morning, Gina and Jalnu prepared their supplies carefully, packing the vaccines in ice to preserve their integrity. Gina had a small bag of supplies and her swag. Jalnu had not packed any belongings. Oh, to travel so lightly! Gina loved the way they just jumped on a plane. How wonderful to travel with so little baggage—physical or emotional.

Chapter Twenty-One

Their arrival was greeted with great excitement. Welcoming faces ushered them into the back of the truck for the short journey from the strip to the camp.

Jalnu and Gina busied themselves giving injections and checking children's hearing and eyesight. Gina also talked with the women and urged them to come in to the clinic next time they were in town to have a Pap smear. Jalnu was invaluable in helping explain the importance of this procedures. She had Gina in stitches as she animatedly explained how to check their breasts for lumps. Every adult was checked for diabetes and signs of other chronic diseases. Diabetes was less of an issue for outstation Aboriginals than for those in communities. They were generally healthier because they still hunted for food and ate very little processed carbohydrate.

As darkness fell, Nanderra, Regan, and the menfolk built a magnificent fire. When it had transformed into glowing embers, the cooking of the feast began. Gina had brought her camp oven to cook the veggies, and they roasted three legs of lamb on a makeshift spit. Dessert consisted of canned peaches and custard, served in disposable bowls with plastic spoons—a great treat for people who knew little of this type of fare. The kids were rapturous, and Gina enjoyed watching their delight.

It had been a long day. When Gina made moves to depart, Nanderra offered to walk her and Regan to the sacred place. They collected their swags and knapsacks and filled up their water bottles from the waterhole. They bid everyone goodnight, and followed

Nanderra into the darkness. Even with a bright moon overhead, Gina had trouble following his sure footsteps. She stumbled more than once and was grateful for Regan's steadying hand behind her.

"Sinkhole over dat way." Nanderra pointed with a jut of his chin in a southerly direction. "Be careful not to wander in the dark. That serpent would enjoy white fella meat fallin' from sky." He chuckled at his attempt at humour. They set up their swags and Nanderra waved goodbye. "I come back when the sun is high," he said. Gina knew these people bedded down late and slept late, and Nanderra would probably come back around midday. "No walking over dat way in the dark, that big sinkhole there. Look when sun wakes up." He instructed, pointing in a southerly direction.

Gina was tired and settled into her swag. She lay on her back and watched the night lights. She wondered how Marc had fared after his rapid departure. She thought about Savannah and whether she would want to return to Lumbarta Island following her reunion with Aiden and her friends in the big smoke.

"The stars are spectacular," Regan said, interrupting her thoughts. "I have never seen a night sky like you see here. It is breathtakingly beautiful."

"It is, indeed."

Together they identified the constellations of the southern sky— the Southern Cross, the Milky Way, the Saucepan. Gina felt weird lying near such a strikingly attractive young man out in the middle of nowhere—but she also felt safe and nurtured.

"So tell me about the special someone in your life," she prodded. "Do you miss them? It must be hard, for you, living this way. There's not many unattached young women around."

"Mmm—let me see. First, there's no special someone except my mum, who I miss heaps. I know that sounds sooky coming from a big guy like me, but I admire and respect her tremendously. I wouldn't be here if she hadn't encouraged me to follow my dreams. I've dreamed of flying for as long as I can remember. Flying is magic. Being here means I'm on track to a commercial licence. I want to lie under the stars all over the world, so this is magic. Wherever life takes me, *this* night sky will remain indelible and most likely be unsurpassed."

"I have lots of friends, but most of all, I want to travel. I want to see the world and hope that I may be fortunate enough to again lie beside a beautiful woman under the roof of the world."

Gina's heart skipped a beat. She was very thankful that the darkness hid her face—she was blushing like a schoolgirl.

Regan continued, "I love being outdoors. I love the Territory, the clear night skies and its deeply contrasting, rugged landscape. I love having the opportunity to visit this sacred place where few white fellas will ever venture. Thank you for allowing me to come along and share this experience with you."

Gina relaxed, fighting sleep, still a little unsettled by his reference to her. *What a charming young man*, she mused. She let his comment drift away as sleep consumed her senses and slowed her breathing.

Chapter Twenty-Two

The early morning sunlight woke Gina. The brighter stars were still watching over them as the warmth brushed her cheeks and filtered its heat into her exposed legs.

She looked across at Regan, who was in a deep sleep. His dark hair was tousled over his face, and his long legs protruded from the light sheet covering his torso. He was indeed a fine-looking young man, and she felt a faint twinge of pride which arose from a place she didn't understand. How privileged was she to be sharing this special place with such a beautiful man? She felt that somehow she had cheated a younger woman out of an experience.

He remained unresponsive to her movements as she quietly rose and began to stroll off towards the sinkhole near their camp. The view from its edge was breathtaking. The sinkhole was deeper than she could have imagined; the tall gums at the bottom and those dotted at various levels on the sides of the hole looked like dwarf shrubs against its red terraces. The water was a deep aquamarine, covering an area about the size of a football field.

By contrast, the cliffs that surrounded their camp were almost as high as the sinkhole was deep. She wondered whether Jalnu's excited imagination had overstated the beauty and "magic" of their caves. The camp and surrounding shrubs were not unlike the remainder of the island. The notion of a nearby utopia was difficult to imagine.

A bush track was readily discernible. Gina began the gentle climb towards the rock face that had, at some point, catapulted itself into life. The morning light captured the red, blue, and gold hues of the rock's variable textures, highlighting their rich autumn shades. Approaching the rock face, the track appeared to disappear. Gina was sure she would run into a dead end. As she came closer, a line of rock folded back on itself, heralding a concealed entrance. Gina moved forward with reverence and entered what she knew must be the sacred place of Nanderra's people.

The walls of the rock antechamber formed the canvas for many a story told over many centuries. Gina marvelled at the exquisitely preserved artwork. She wondered at the history it recorded. Why were many of the people depicted with halos or helmets? Could this be a story of an alien visit in times past?

She noticed the decrease in temperature immediately; the further she ventured, the cooler it became. Relief from the heat was magic. Gina passed through two antechambers, admiring their beauty— Jalnu had not exaggerated. The parched exterior landscape had given way to passages of fern-draped walls glistening with natural water seepage and dappled sunlight. The odour and damp permeated her senses. Below on a sandy bed ran a stream so clear she had to ripple the surface with her hand to confirm its presence. Gina bent to drink the water. It was cool and pure and seemed to vitalise her whole body.

A small bend in the passageway hinted at a larger chamber. She stood in awe of the scene that unfolded as she turned the corner. A large emerald-green pool touched the sand where she stood, spreading out to meet the sides of the chamber. A narrow waterfall spilled from the grotto's ceiling into the water below, trickling down the rear rock face. As the water fell, it separated into diamond droplets. At the far end of the chamber, the pooled water was turned light green by a shaft of sunlight that pierced its serene surface.

Gina felt like an intruder on nature's majesty. At the same time, she felt compelled to become part of it. Mesmerised by this magnificent place, she slowly unbuttoned her shirt and let it slide from her shoulders. She unzipped her shorts, stepping out of them as they fell to her ankles. Her bra and panties came off with equal abandon, and she waded into the enticing water. Her body slowly sank into its greenness. She began to relax as the coolness homogenised her body heat. She waded towards the waterfall and its shaft of light, the water gradually reaching the crests of her hips.

As she approached the sunlight, she was bathed by the mist of falling water. Her whole body tingled as she soaked up a spiritual experience she had never before encountered. It was as if the whole world had stopped and transcended her physical being. If there was a heaven, this must be part of it, she decided. Not even the disturbance of the water behind her could raise her from this state of euphoria.

Dawning awareness brought her to the realisation that someone else shared her space. She slowly turned to see the taut young body of Regan, fully naked and aroused. She moved towards him as if in a trance. She reached up to fold her arms around his shoulders. Her breasts tingled as they caressed his impressive chest. His hands gently explored her back and then moved down to cup her bottom. He gently lifted her. They kissed deeply as passion overtook them both. He eased her onto himself, and together they generated the rhythm of lovemaking. Gina could feel the warmth of the sunlight on her back.

She felt exhilarated, any thoughts of protest were absent. Not one muscle fibre would respond to Gina's feeble conscience that bleated this could not happen. Instead her body moved in defiance of her sense of propriety, smothered by his fervent, moist, deep kisses. Regan made love to her with the passion of youth and a majesty beyond his years.

"Not a word," Regan cautioned when they made love again on the cool golden sands of the chamber. "Just love me."

And she did.

Chapter Twenty-Three

Following their visit to the cave Gina had led Regan to the sinkhole and together they stood in stunned silence, in awe of its magnificence. Time stood still.

Regan and Gina greeted Nanderra as he walked towards them. The sun was now high. Upon his arrival Nanderra was particularly chummy and nudged Regan as he approached. Gina decided it was a transcultural *blokey* thing and chose to ignore its innuendo.

They returned to the outstation, and Regan prepared the plane for take-off. Jalnu approached Gina, stopping in her tracks she eyed Gina suspiciously. She then began to giggle and sidled up to her. "Your secret OK with me. I told you them caves are magic. Younger man good, nah?"

Gina's shocked face confirmed what Jalnu had already guessed. Jalnu's tone was neither accusatory nor judgemental, just matter-of-fact. But it frightened Gina to think that she was so transparent. Would the whole world know of her morning of passion? She thought not. *Damn the intuitive consciousness of these people*, she thought as she reproached herself.

It was a quiet flight back to the community, and an even more awkward silence after they had dropped Jalnu off at her camp. Gina brought the vehicle to a halt outside of Regan's house and offered a curt goodbye. Regan turned to her. "Don't do this, Gina. I have no regrets about this morning, and I hope you won't either. We are two consenting adults who have hurt no one and who hold each other in high regard. Nothing else matters."

Gina managed a partial but uncomfortable smile and drove away. Alexa's words again emerged from her consciousness: "A quick fuck from a young buck." Was that all it had been? Had this happened at her invitation? What on earth had she been thinking?

After unloading the equipment at the clinic, Gina returned to her flat. She was afraid that anyone she might meet would see in her what had been so obvious to Jalnu and Nanderra, and she was suddenly very tired.

She felt ashamed and guilty. How could she lecture Savannah on the rights and wrongs of relationships? How could she face Regan again? Did he think she was just a lonely old woman and therefore an easy lay? Had he been repulsed by her ageing body? At the very least, he probably felt sorry for her.

The strongest component of her guilt was the fact that she had enjoyed the moment beyond words. It had stirred a depth of desire she had never before experienced and had been sure would always elude her. Perhaps she *was* desperate for someone to hold her, to make love to her, to make her feel desired, to reignite the passion she thought long lost.

Gina lay on her bed with the fan rotating at full speed, the pulses of air brushing away her recriminations. She acknowledged her guilt but had no regrets.

Savannah was due to return from her holiday at the end of the week. Gina wondered if she would return. It would be difficult after being in the city. Savannah had not yet confirmed her flight details, and this worried Gina. So too did the fact that she was unsure about how she would react when she next encountered Regan. She was afraid that Savannah might tune in to her discomfort—she had never been good at hiding her feelings from Savannah.

By the end of the week, Savannah had radioed to let her know she would be in on the morning flight the following Sunday.

"I'm so relieved," said Gina. "I was afraid you had decided to stay, and I'm not ready to have you leave the nest just yet."

"You left the nest, Mum, not me. I did have reservations about coming back, but I need … I've got some stuff to take care of. And besides, Dad's coming back with me. It will be great."

Oh no, thought Gina. *I'm just not ready to handle him too.* She was aghast but managed to salvage her reaction sufficiently. "That's great, love. But do you *really* think Dad's ready to cope with all of this? He's definitely a city lad now, you know."

"He'll be fine, Mum. He's looking forward to seeing where you work—and you."

Gina sank down on the chair near the radio and repeated, "That's great. I'll see you soon, honey." She felt too confused to deal with Savannah's attempts at matchmaking, and was afraid that Aiden might have construed her agreeing to his visit as a sign of her interest in reconciliation.

Gina knew that Savannah's unfinished business involved Balunn but chose not to comment further. Conversations on the radio would be heard all over the Territory, and she was still reeling at the news of Aiden's imminent visit.

Savannah had spent her leave catching up with her friends and enjoying Aiden's undivided attention. She congratulated him on his efforts to tone up and look after himself better. She also broached the possibility that those efforts might be due to the influence of another woman. Aiden had dismissed this line of discussion so adamantly that she didn't raise it again until three days before her proposed return.

She and Aiden sat in the solarium, absorbing the warmth of the winter sun and protected from the icy winds. The aroma of sweetened hot chocolate permeated the air. Savannah plucked up the courage to ask Aiden about his relationship with Gina. She wanted to know why they had drifted apart. It was obvious that they still held each other in high regard. Why didn't they make a move to reconcile?

Aiden answered her as honestly as he could, admitting his large part in their separation and how much his drinking and its associated behaviour had influenced their marital journey. "I'll always be sorry I couldn't see what was happening before it was too late."

"Is it too late, Dad? I know Mum still thinks a lot of you. Isn't it worth a try? Why don't you come back with me? You've still got another two weeks' leave. Maybe if you come back and see why Mum's work means so much to her, you will be able to reach a compromise."

"I don't think so. I appreciate your suggestion, but I really think it's too late. Too much water under the bridge now."

Gina was glad not to be on call on the day of Savannah's arrival. It was a beautiful, crisp morning, and she decided to take a walk along the beach to quiet her welling excitement. As she walked, three young children joined her and barraged her with their usual questions about all things, personal and otherwise.

One of the leather dogs accompanied them. It was a brown dog and still had most of its hair—probably a cross kelpie, and no more than six months old. The dog frolicked and romped with the kids as they skipped along beside her. Gina inquired as to its name and was told, "Brown Dog." She laughed. What an apt name. It was the first community dog not to growl at her and bare its teeth. No doubt it was too young to follow the example of the other dogs.

Gina enjoyed her newfound company very much. Their endless chatter and timeless enjoyment of simplicity amused her. They were a delight.

She heard a plane overhead and knew Savannah was almost home. It would be nice to see Aiden again, but an afternoon at the Coffee Corner in central Brunswick would have sufficed.

Regan was the pilot on duty that day, so Savannah enjoyed both the internal and external view from the plane.

"Look, Savannah, there's your mum!" Regan exclaimed in a manner that was alarmingly enthusiastic. He made a low swoop over the beach, tipping the wing to wave to Gina. He then set the plane in a vertical climb higher than Savannah had ever been in a small plane. He looped backwards, gliding over the group of beach walkers.

"Are you *crazy*? What are you trying to do, kill us?" screamed Savannah. Aiden was speechless, pale, and feeling ill—he couldn't even summon enough energy to voice his protest.

Gina too watched the daredevil stunt and was angry at Regan for risking her daughter's life. She was also flattered beyond belief. How would she explain this to Aiden and Savannah?

She and Regan had seen each other twice since their interlude at the caves. Afternoons on the veranda included playing cards or draughts, coupled with stimulating conversation. They had agreed that lovemaking must not happen again. They enjoyed each other's company tremendously. Gina had to keep reminding herself of their age difference. This was compounded during one of their many conversations when she learned that Regan's parents were a couple of years younger than her. She constantly questioned their friendship, knowing that if her son had survived, she would not be happy were he to engage in a relationship such as this.

Regan had scoffed at her protestations and assured her that it was no one else's business but theirs. He was charming and respectful, acceding to their pact that an ongoing physical relationship was not an option.

As Gina watched the plane circle over the flat, she felt sick at the thought of Aiden's impending visit. She knew she had probably given him a message of hope when, from her perspective, there was none.

Gina ran up to the clinic to get the health truck and bounced her way out to the airport to collect Savannah and Aiden. Gina and Savannah embraced warmly—they had missed each other. Gina, feeling very uncomfortable, then reservedly embraced Aiden. She cast a look over his shoulder, past Savannah, to catch Regan smiling at her in a way that suggested conspiracy.

Gina, Aiden, and Savannah climbed into the truck and headed back on the rickety road to town. "Tell me about the city. How is everyone?" Gina inquired.

Savannah launched into a day-by-day, event-by-event description of her holiday. Aiden sat quietly stunned at the picture unfolding as they approached the township—the derelict buildings, the lack of industrious activity, and, in contrast, the merriment of the children.

"So did you meet anyone you love more than yourself?" teased Gina.

"Nah. The guys from school are still there, and they're still good friends. No one of any interest. So, what do you reckon, Dad? Is it different from anywhere you've ever been?"

"It does remind me of some of my Asian jaunts, except the terrain is much more barren," replied Aiden.

"How's Balunn? Have you seen much of him?" Savannah ventured.

"Yes. He's been spending quite a lot of time with Mandy. They make a good couple," Gina baited her, until she saw the look of disappointment on Savannah's face. Gina broke into a smile. "Hey, babe, I'm just kidding. I don't know what he's been up to. We did have a bit of trouble while you were away, and I was sure glad to see him that day." She went on to relate the story of Karundi's shooting and Marc's eviction from the community. "It was all pretty scary when it happened, but in hindsight it couldn't have happened to a nicer person. Karundi has been a lot quieter and more respectful since then."

She changed the subject. "I'm glad you're back today because I have to fly to Darwin tomorrow for a seminar. I'll be back on Wednesday. You'll have to look after your dad for a couple of days."

Both Savannah and Aiden looked disappointed. Savannah managed to rally first. "Sure, Mum. I've got lots of work to do. I feel very safe here, and now I've got my dad to keep the bogeys away. It'll be great, Dad. We'll go to the swimming hole—it's beautiful. I'll show you how to catch a barramundi Aboriginal style."

As they pulled up at the clinic, Savannah's heart skipped a beat. There was Balunn, waiting for her. He was seated on the veranda steps as if he had been there since the day she left.

"We'll take the bags down to the flat," Gina offered, knowing that she and Aiden were not the company that the younger couple wanted just now.

"Thanks, Mum. Balunn and I might go for a walk out to the jetty landing."

Gina introduced Aiden to Balunn. He shot out a hand of greeting and said he was honoured to meet Savannah's father. Aiden reluctantly shook his hand, eyeing him suspiciously but also pleasantly surprised at his well-mannered, articulate response. Balunn and Savannah set off down the road. Aiden's stare following them as they chatted, obviously relaxed in each other's company.

Gina wondered why she was becoming an accomplice to a relationship she had warned Savannah against. The truth was that she liked Balunn very much. She knew he had some wonderful and amiable qualities. But the concept of her daughter having any future with him was unthinkable. She also knew Aiden would find any suggestion of a relationship between Savannah and Balunn unpalatable. She told herself they were too young to have a serious relationship—then reprimanded herself. She had met her first love when she was younger than Savannah, and she remembered the depth of intensity she had felt.

"What's with the black kid?" Aiden wanted to know.

"He and Savannah are friends. Balunn is a lovely person, and more than that I do not wish to discuss. He helped Savannah enormously with her maths, hence her brilliant grade. Savannah is old enough to choose her friends. I am proud that their colour is not one of the criteria she uses to choose her friends," Gina replied a little too caustically.

Chapter Twenty-Four

Aiden and Gina were about to ascend the stairway to her flat when Regan pulled his motorbike to a halt by the gate. "Regan Ayres, I'm gonna punch your face in, you bloody show-off. How dare you try those sort of stunts with my precious daughter and her father on board?" Gina threatened with all the anger she could muster.

Gina made a point of explaining that Aiden would be staying in the third flat, and that he needed to have a lie-down as he was feeling ill—no thanks to the dangerous antics of irresponsible pilots on top of his natural fear of flying.

"Sorry about that. You should have yelled out. I didn't realise you were squeamish about flying. A guy has to do something for excitement up here. See you both later!"

Aiden grunted, trying his best to appear unaffected by his delicate position. Regan mounted his bike and sped off towards home.

Gina made Aiden a cup of tea, which helped calm his jaded nerves a little. Then she escorted him to his flat, turning on the air conditioner so that he could rest in comfort. She promised to call him for dinner.

No sooner had she settled Aiden into his room and returned to her flat than Regan reappeared. He burst into a raucous laughter, pushing her backwards beyond the doorway of her flat. He continued to laugh as he pushed her onto the bed.

"What are you doing, Regan? We agreed—"

His kisses swallowed her words. "I love that you're *angry*, great performance" he murmured against her lips.

"What if Savannah or Aiden come back?" Gina protested.

"Tell me not to do this and I'll stop." He paused. She said nothing. "That was the best stunt I've ever pulled. It got you all fired up, didn't it?"

"You're an arrogant, self-centred arsehole." She relaxed into his embrace and they explored the sexual tension they had amassed and tried so hard to stifle.

"I knew you weren't mad. We'll have fun in Darwin—just you and me."

"What do you mean, 'we'?"

"I've arranged a couple of days off. Thought I'd show you the highlights of the top end."

"That's somewhat presumptuous of you," said Gina with feigned indignation.

As dusk began to settle, Regan kissed Gina goodbye. "See you bright and early in the morning. Seven o'clock sharp, OK?"

Gina found it hard to contain her excitement. Conference aside, it would be wonderful to have some unscrutinised time together. She felt only a little guilty at leaving Aiden behind and was glad to have a reason to escape from his intensity and unspoken expectations. There were no prizes for guessing the agenda for Aiden's visit, the resumption of their relationship being the obvious goal.

Gina showered and began to prepare dinner. Not wanting to spend time alone with Aiden, she would wake him when Savannah returned.

Savannah and Balunn reached the jetty landing and sat side by side with their legs dangling over the edge. The old wooden structure was as sturdy as the day it had been built. The clear blue-green waters, ebbing and flowing with the tide, had done little to undermine its integrity.

"Aren't you afraid of the salty lizards?" Savannah asked with sincerity.

"Not today—they're upriver," replied Balunn authoritatively.

"How can you be so sure?"

"It's just that time of year. They head upstream to breed."

She felt a little nervous but sat close to Balunn, their arms and thighs touching. A current circuited between them that was unmistakably circular.

"I missed you, Balunn. I tried hard not to, but I did," ventured Savannah.

He put his arm around her and pulled her close. "I was afraid you wouldn't come back. Before you left, I stayed away to give you the space to make that decision without any pressure. I love you, Savannah."

He stated his feelings simply, unafraid of rejection but concerned for her position. She turned to him, and they kissed and then embraced desperately. "I'm scared," she whispered. "What's going to happen to us? It's not long before I go back to Melbourne for the Christmas break and for good … and then I'm off to uni for three or four years."

"I know. I've thought about it a lot, but I can't see a way around it. Our people are depending on me. I have been raised with a great sense of responsibility, and I feel I must not let my people down. There is an expectation that I will follow in my father's footsteps."

Savannah lay her head on his shoulder. She felt happy to be held and sad about the inevitability of their parting. They sat and talked until well after sundown.

Dinner was almost ready when Savannah walked into Gina's flat. Gina was humming happily as she put the final touches to the meal. She didn't notice when Savannah sat quietly and unobtrusively on a kitchen chair. Savannah watched Gina and wondered at her demeanour—it was a happy mood, but there was something more. She secretly hoped it was due to Aiden's arrival, but, gauging from her cordial but cool behaviour towards him, Savannah suspected another reason.

Gina was acting like a schoolgirl in love.

As Savannah observed her mum, she realised that this was closer to the truth than she had first thought. Regan's aerobatics, his not-so-subtle joy in spotting Gina on the beach, the preoccupied hug Gina had given Aiden at the airport, and now something else that Savannah didn't care to think too deeply about—what on earth was her mother thinking? Savannah tried to dismiss the thought. Regan and her mother? No way.

Gina turned, steaming hot saucepan in hand, and for the first time noticed Savannah's presence. "Hi, honey. Don't you just love this cooler weather? It feels so clean and fresh here—no smog, no traffic noise, no sirens, no TV. It's great, isn't it?" She smiled.

Savannah's face was deadpan. "What's going on, Mum?"

"What—what do you mean?" asked Gina defensively.

"I think you know what I mean. What's with you and Regan Ayres?"

"Why do you ask?" When cornered, Gina's response was always to answer with a question.

"I can't believe this. I just can't believe it. How dare you lecture me on my relationships and have it off with a guy young enough to be your son? How could you? Why didn't you tell me before Dad came up? He's come all this way to see you!" Savannah stormed out of the flat.

Gina didn't respond to her accusations—she thought it best not to go near this topic. She called after Savannah, "Fetch your father for dinner."

Chapter Twenty-Five

At seven the next morning, Regan, Gina, and a local family of three soared into the perfect blue sky. Gina was tired. She had hardly slept, excited by the prospect of their stolen days together but deeply troubled by the hurt she had caused Savannah. She had been right about Savannah's ability to read her— spot on this time. She was also annoyed that she had agreed to Aiden's visit. His presence merely compounded her guilt and complicated her life.

Three hours later, they arrived in Darwin, secured the plane, and headed into the city. Gina had made a pact with herself to enjoy the moment ... and she did. She and Regan had lunch at an Italian al fresco restaurant located on bay of the harbour and shopped all afternoon. The best and worst thing about living in a community was that there was nowhere and nothing on which to spend one's money. They both enjoyed their shopping frenzy very much. "We're like two bulls in a china shop!" Gina laughed.

"You can be the cow. I'll be the bull," joked Regan, thoroughly enjoying Gina's exuberance.

"I'm exhausted," said Gina as they got back to the hotel, laden with shopping bags.

"Tell you what," said Regan. "I've got to go to head office to sort out some paperwork. I've nearly got my hours up for my full commercial licence. You have a rest, and I'll be back by seven. We'll go out for dinner. Deal?"

"Sounds fantastic." Gina kissed him on the cheek as he left.

The spa bath looked very inviting, but she opted for a shower. It was wonderful not having to worry about how much water she used. She lingered there for a full twenty minutes before climbing into bed. She decided to ring Alexa purely to enjoy the luxury of a private phone call.

Alexa answered after the third ring. It was good to hear her voice. They chatted with the ease of lifelong companions about anything and everything. Before she realised it, Gina was relating her affair with Regan. She had not intended to tell Alexa but knew she would not be admonished, even though part of her needed to be. Another part of her just had to share her joy with someone.

"You go, girl! Enjoy—we're a long time dead," was the best advice Alexa could offer.

"You're not much help. I need to be scolded to appease my religious upbringing—but I guess that's also the reason I've told you and no one else."

Gina hung up the phone, happy to have talked so freely. The crisp white sheets, which were laundered to perfection, melded into her body and soon seduced her into sleep.

She was awakened by the warmth of Regan's body nestling into her back. She loved her back being caressed and knew that it was the most sensual part of her being. They made love, hungrily. Champagne kisses and naked bodies complimented the luxury of knowing, for the first time, that their time together was, for now, limitless, unobserved.

The evening brought with it the magic of a Darwin light show. The curtains of their third-floor unit were wide open and framed the magnificent dance of top-end lightning splitting the voluptuous grey clouds emerging out of the blue-grey ocean.

Gina was revelling in her contentment when Regan returned from the bathroom and invited her to join him. The spa bath was full, and the aroma of jasmine wafted through the air. The surrounds of the bath were decorated with lighted candles and small bowls of freshly cut fruit. Gina exclaimed, "I'm overwhelmed! You're amazing!

This is the most wonderful thing anyone has ever done for me. You are a romantic genius, and I love you."

Together they climbed into the bath, massaging and loving each other unreservedly. Hunger eventually overtook passion, and they dressed for dinner. At the restaurant, they were escorted to a corner table by the window. In the eerie darkness of the storm's aftermath, the stillness of the ocean was sensed rather than seen. Regan held Gina's hand. He was proud of his companion. Their love was palpable to the point that they became aware of the stares of people around them.

Their waiter, whose name badge read *Timothy*, was obviously intrigued by them. He was overattentive and not particularly discreet in trying to view Gina's left hand. Gina and Regan made this their evening entertainment and teased him mercilessly, giving him conflicting snippets of information about their relationship. By the end of their delightful dinner, they could see Timothy was just about beside himself with curiosity. Regan tipped him generously, then deliberately embraced Gina as they waited for him to settle their account. This further piqued Timothy's intrigue and put a fitting end to their night's entertainment.

Gina spent the following day at the conference while Regan caught up with friends. They knew this night would not emulate the previous night. There was some serious talking to be done, and both wanted to stall the inevitable.

But Gina's encroaching dread could be stilled no longer. Why did she feel like this when she had just experienced the most wonderful night of her life? She finally broached the subject both had tried valiantly to avoid. "This can't go on, Regan. We both know that."

"I know, but it doesn't have to end yet. Let's wait and see what happens."

"I can't. I'm already in love with you. Prolonging this can only result in the destruction of what has become sacred to me. Either way, one or both of us will be deeply hurt. I am already devastated by the thought of not seeing you again, but this is something we need to do—and quickly. I want you to ask for a transfer. Your time on the island is nearly up anyway. You said yesterday that you are close to having all your flying hours up."

Gina felt so very sad and looked to Regan for support.

"Is this about Savannah finding out?"

"No, not entirely … Well, it's a little bit about her but mostly about us. Regan, I find you irresistible, but I have no right to be with you. You are young and have your entire life ahead of you. I can never be part of it. You cannot introduce me to your friends or to your family. Our life would always be cloak and dagger stuff, and we both deserve better than that. Mostly I'd be taking up your time, monopolising your young life when you should be forming a relationship with someone who can share your whole life, bear your children, and live your dreams. I have had all these things and cannot see you robbed of any of this. I love you too much."

Reluctant tears escaped her eyes and cascaded down her cheeks. Gina had committed the ultimate sin—she was not sorry but felt incredibly selfish. "I wish you nothing but a good life. I am so grateful that you have given me this short time together, this special part of you that I will always cherish. It has been the most wonderful, most passionate time of my life. I will ever be indebted to you for including me as one of the special people in your life. You make me feel beautiful and loved. You roused a level of passion in me that I never knew existed."

Regan moved towards Gina to comfort her. She put her hand up in a stop signal. He continued anyway and sat beside her. "It seems to me that somehow you need to lay blame, and so you are blaming yourself for allowing this to happen. Please don't, Gina. I'm a man with a man's will, a man's heart, and a man's feelings. I may be young, but I know enough of life to know love, and I love you. This is not your decision alone. I have a major stake in this. Don't dismiss me. Don't cheapen the depth of feelings I have for you."

"Please don't make this any harder than it is. It is the hardest thing I have ever had to do. Leaving someone out of love is much harder that leaving someone you no longer love. You will meet someone special because you are special.

"I've booked to fly back with NT Airlines as far as Nhulunbuy tomorrow. Can we just spend this one last night together? I want you to hold me. I want you to know that you are so very special and I feel privileged to be close to you. Our time has been so short but has devoured my heart and soul."

They held each other and sobbed. They both knew there was no other option.

The following day, Gina left Darwin for Nhulunbuy. She felt devastated.

As she walked the familiar hospital corridors to Carmen's office, she went through the motions of greeting those she knew. She felt she was in a vacuum. The corridor felt like waves that seemed to be moving with each step. She knocked on Carmen's door and entered before the invitation was extended.

"Hi, Gina! Good to see you. How was the conference?" Carmen asked, pleased to see her friend.

Gina burst into tears.

Carmen came around her desk and steered Gina to the lounge. She held Gina while Gina sobbed and sobbed and sobbed. Carmen knew this was not a time to talk.

Some ten minutes later, Gina's sobs subsided into a part cry, part sniffle.

"What on earth has happened?" Carmen asked. "Is Savannah OK?"

Gina nodded her head.

"Has something happened to your family? What is it?"

Gina sniffled and wiped her eyes and nose for another five minutes before she could answer. "Carmen, I've fallen in love," she sobbed.

Carmen started to laugh. "Oh my God, that's wonderful! I

thought someone must have died or something." She stopped and looked at Gina's demeanour and knew that it didn't fit the words she had uttered. "What is it, Gina? Surely this is a good thing—is it not? He doesn't love you?"

"Yes, he does but … No, it's not a good thing. Our love just can't be."

"I don't want to pry, but surely it can't be that bad. What's the problem? Is he gay?"

"No."

"Is he a priest? Is this person a woman?"

"No and no. I can't tell you except to say that he is the most wonderful thing that has ever happened to me. I should feel deep shame, but I just feel empty. I can't tell you any more than that."

Gina again began to cry. Carmen slid in behind her and hugged her. She rocked Gina like a baby. "I can't comprehend any situation where mutual love can bring this much pain."

Gina stopped and, for the first time, realised the cause of her deep pain. She looked at Carmen and quietly stated, "I'm in love with my son."

Chapter Twenty-Six

Regan booked out of the hotel. He sat for some time in the hire car. He felt like all the energy he had possessed had drained from his body. He breathed in, deeply conscious that he was inhaling Gina's scent. He could feel her presence, hear her laughter—this was going to be a long, hard day.

He turned the ignition and headed towards the airport. Tears rolled down his face.

How could anything that felt so right be so wrong? The whole world felt wrong. He pulled over on the oceanfront promenade and sat looking blankly out across the bay. It too seemed to have lost its beauty.

Regan despaired. Would he ever be able to recapture what he and Gina had shared? Their relationship had eclipsed any he had previously known. The mutual respect, trust, and honesty they shared had evolved over a short duration, catapulting their love into unknown territory. They had reached a spiritual connection that Regan had previously believed was only seeded and nourished in romantic fiction.

He watched two young women walk past. They wore short shorts and skimpy tops—a sight that would normally have attracted his considerable interest. Not today. They seemed like silly young girls. He felt irritated by their light banter and playful attempts to engage his attention.

Life goes on, they say, he thought. *I guess it does, but not today.*

He wheeled the car back into the traffic, narrowly missing

another vehicle. The driver hurled abuse at him and shook his fist as he passed by.

When Regan reached the airport, Marc was outside the office building. He bounded up as Regan walked towards the office. "Hey, mate, great seeing you again. I didn't know you were in Darwin. When are— What the hell's the matter with you?"

"Nothing," Regan responded dismissively.

"It must be a bloody big nothing. You look like someone's just stolen your teddy bear!"

Regan reeled towards Marc. "Shut the fuck up"

Holding up his hands in a defensive gesture, Marc said "Whoa, hold up, matey. Whatever it is, you obviously don't wanna talk about it. Sorry I asked."

"You got that right."

Regan brushed Marc aside and walked through the office, past the administrative assistant, and straight into his boss's office. He sat down heavily and announced that he wasn't going back to the community. He wanted out of the Territory. He was confident he had enough hours to land himself a job back in Western Australia and that's where he'd be heading—today.

His boss inquired as to the problem.

"Family problems. I need to go back home; they need me." He didn't offer any further explanation.

Sensing his distress, his boss asked if he could help.

"Nah. Thanks, but no. I just need to go home. Sorry to dump this on you with no notice."

Regan had been a great worker. He could fly as well as any of the young pilots Ted Farmer had trained and better than most. Ted was concerned for his young protégé—he had never before been privy to this side of Regan. Ted was a solidly built, balding man who was as fit as any man his age. Regan thought he was probably in his mid to late forties. He had keen brown eyes and an entertaining Australian drawl, coupled with a keen Irish wit. He was also one of the best instructors Regan had ever worked with. For his friendship, knowledge, and concern, Regan was grateful.

"Sure. mate. You go. There's always some other snotty-nosed kid chomping at the bit to take your place. But if ever you need a job, let me know. There's a flight to Perth this arvo—want me to see if I can get you a berth?"

Regan calmed at his concern. "Yeah, I'd appreciate it. Thanks."

"Whatever the problem, hope things work out OK for you, mate."

Regan had liked Ted from the first moment they met. He felt obligated to him and hated himself for letting him down. Ted had employed Regan over twenty-nine other applicants keen to get a start in commercial flying. He was grateful that Ted had the good sense not to delve into the real reasons for his departure. He knew Ted had guessed there was more to this sudden decision. "Thanks again, mate. Can't talk, just got to go. Thanks for everything."

Regan shook Ted's hand, turned, and left the office. He knew that he would dissolve into tears if he had to endure any more of Ted's kindness—better to leave while his composure was still intact.

Chapter Twenty-Seven

Carmen was dismayed.

She sat quietly rocking Gina, trying to comprehend Gina's revelation. What son? Gina had no son.

Gina began to explain. Carmen resisted the urge to interrupt, to ask the myriad of questions that bombarded her mind. As Gina ventured deeper into her story, Carmen was transfixed. Gina was grateful for the trust she knew in Carmen; it finally allowed her to tell her story from beginning to end for the first time in her life.

In telling her story, Gina became poignantly aware that someone else deserved an explanation. She felt calm after talking with Carmen. She left the office, went to her room, and began to write.

> *Dearest Regan, my love—*
>
> *I sincerely hope I can explain so that we can both better comprehend the events of the past weeks.*
>
> *For my entire life I have carried the pain of loss, as do many. However, the pain of losing of my son was something I have never come to terms with. You have helped me do that.*
>
> *As a young girl, I was whisked away from my country origins into the world of modelling. I fell in love and became pregnant. Sadly, this love was not returned. While working on a photo shoot in central Australia, I miscarried. I have never dealt with that*

pain. I concealed the pregnancy and, along with it, my grief.

Strangely, though, my son led me to my present career and ultimately to you. It was through my loss that I came to yearn to work with indigenous Australians in this remote part of the world. To do my small part to help, to try to repay the kindness the indigenous women once showed a stranger, a white fella in distress. To these women I owe my ability to cope. These women, who spoke very little English, showed me unconditional love—more than I had ever known. They knew the importance of me holding my baby, of saying hello and then goodbye.

I never spoke of my miscarriage except in a very general sense and only to my friend Alexis. I was never able to tell others because the pain was too personal, the experience too lonely to share with anyone who might not understand.

I cannot impress upon you enough the huge part you have played in my healing. You have allowed me to love my son and release him—to let the grief dissipate. To you I owe the resolution of my grief, the remainder of my recovery.

You have also featured prominently in helping me to understand what has driven me, why I have felt the winds of discontent so often throughout my adult years, and for that I also thank you.

Something greater than ourselves drew us together. Maybe you are my son's spirit, but I know you are not my son. I have never before felt so truly loved, so cocooned against the impediments of the world, so very special.

I wish you a happy life, Regan. If you were my son's spirit, I could not have asked for a more beautiful son. I could not have been more proud than I would have been if you were of my body. Again, I must love and release.

I know you will find happiness because you are special. Someone special awaits you.

I thank you with all my heart.

I named my son Regan Jai.

Forever grateful, forever loving—Gina

Chapter Twenty-Eight

Although Gina returned to Lumbarta Island that afternoon, it was months before she could bring herself to talk with Savannah about her relationship with Regan. She had not talked to anyone but Carmen about its demise. She missed him so much. She felt angry that their wonderful time had been short-lived, and yet grateful to have found her way through him.

Initially Gina found it very difficult to hide her sorrow. She felt despondent. It was hard to keep her composure and focus. Every plane she heard was Regan's. The sound of an engine tore at her heart. She couldn't help but hope Regan would be its pilot.

Aiden's presence had made it more difficult. He too knew her well enough to see that she was unhappy. He offered for her to come back to Melbourne, thinking the cause of her despondency might be her workload. Of course, he secretly hoped that this might increase their chances of reigniting the flame.

Come on, Sunday. Only three days to go, thought Gina. She would be glad to see Aiden leave. He was pleasant company, but reigniting their relationship, as far as Gina was concerned, is out of the question. He spent the next three days conjuring up theories as to why Gina wasn't herself. At one stage he was close to suggesting a broken romance, but he could clearly see that there weren't any local prospects—a view that Gina found particularly offensive. She wasn't sure whether he thought no one would be interested in her or whether he didn't consider that any Aboriginal man had the capacity to hold her interest.

Aiden finally departed. Over the ensuing weeks, conversations between Gina and Savannah were superficial and included only those subjects that Gina deemed safe. It had been a heart-rending divide—she had lost Regan and, along with him, the trust and respect of her daughter. Gina hated not feeling close to Savannah and tried valiantly to rationalise and suppress her sorrow.

Savannah too had had much time to think. She knew that she was angry and a little disgusted with her mother's behaviour. Part of her anger was due to the inevitable outcome of her own relationship with Balunn, and the dashing of her hope that her parents would someday reunite.

She was also shocked. She could not get her head around the idea of her mother being a sexual and sensual woman who was capable of being attractive to such a hot guy. This did not fit with her concept of her mother, nor did it sit well within the confines of her propriety.

Regan had left the community. She didn't know or care where he had gone.

It was the weekend prior to Savannah's final departure from the island. Gina knew she must broach the subject with Savannah. She couldn't bear the thought of their stand-off continuing. Gina's next annual leave was three months away. By then Savannah would have settled into life as a university student.

"Savannah, I know you are still angry at me. I'm sorry to have caused you so much hurt when you're dealing with your own relationship issues. It was never my intention to get close to Regan. It was something that consumed us, even though we both knew it couldn't and shouldn't be. I understand that you are disappointed in me and that I have let you down by discrediting your ideals and expectations. I know too that I've let you down because I have been feeling so sad that I haven't been there for you when you needed me."

"It's OK. Mum. You're right that I felt ashamed of you and angry and let down. Now, I'm not so sure. I still feel those things to a degree, but because I too have found a love destined for failure, I am beginning to understand that we don't have control of our hearts. We only think we do. I'm sorry too, Mum. I'm sorry for both of us. I don't blame you. In fact, part of me is proud of you."

Savannah hugged Gina for a long time. They were both pleased to be talking again—really talking. "What do you mean, 'proud of me'?" Gina asked.

"Well, I figured that not too many people my age have a mum capable of such passion *and* with the ability to pull a guy like Regan Ayres," Savannah teased.

Gina laughed. "Yes, but don't ever think it was pure lust. Maybe that was a big part of it … but it was also very beautiful and ended very painfully."

"I know, Mum. I've not been blind to your sadness. As you're always telling me, it will pass. At least that's what I tell myself."

"How are things with you and Balunn?"

"Not all that much different to your situation. Very hard and very painful. I love him. We've tried to cool it, but it's been so hard. I'll miss him forever," Savannah replied as she hugged Gina tighter.

Savannah's return to Melbourne was very difficult. Her heart was heavy. She would miss Gina, and she had already begun to ache for Balunn. His sparkling eyes, engaging smile, and tender caresses were still vivid memories. She had not seen much of him in the past few weeks. She inquired as to his whereabouts the day before her departure, and was told he had gone walkabout to hunt and fish. Balunn knew she would know why he had gone.

Upon her return to the city, she quickly caught up again with all her friends. She enjoyed a great Christmas together with Aiden and the zany Alexa. She wrote to Balunn every week. Every week he wrote back. She wondered how long it would be before the frequent exchange of letters subsided—which one of them would let go first.

Despite her sadness, the holiday seemed to fly by. It was soon *O* week—orientation at uni. Savannah managed a great score in her final exam, knowing that without Balunn's help, this would not have happened. She still missed him and wondered when the ache in her heart would begin to fade.

She was looking forward to her studies in social work very much. She was excited that her friend Deborah was enrolled in the same course. It would be great to have someone to study with.

After completing their enrolments and attending the lunchtime barbecue offered by the student body, she and Deb decided to explore the uni grounds. The university was close to the city but set in twenty-five acres of lush bushland. The native flora decorated the pathways and lined the creek beds that meandered between the buildings. It was a tranquil setting and one that Savannah felt would inspire her commitment to work hard and help curb her pain.

Deb and she were overawed by the magnitude of the place. They felt they would never find their way from class to class without a detailed map and compass. "Well, forget the compass," said Savannah. "I'd be just as hopeless with one as without one."

They sat down on a small wooden bridge that curved over a shallow bubbling brook and dangled their aching feet in the cool water.

"Watch out for those salty lizards," came a familiar voice from behind them.

Savannah's heart stopped. It could only be Balunn. She leapt to her feet and into his arms in one deft movement.

Deb looked on in amazement, stunned by the magnificence of this handsome black man. She knew, from her many in-depth discussions with Savannah, that this was Balunn. "Shi-it, I know why you had the hots, kiddo," she said as she leant back to take in and admire his commanding presence.

Balunn swept Savannah off her feet literally, cradling her in his arms. He swung her around in a full circle and lifted her higher as he hugged her tightly. "What, how?" Savannah spluttered.

Balunn's face lit up with his smile as wide as the ocean. He answered, "My father is a very wise man. He wants no more sit-down money for his people. He said I must come to further my education. His wish is that I should understand business so we can develop proper enterprise to sustain island industry and restore pride through meaningful work. I am to learn white fella ways so we can deal on white fella terms. He also knows I am too sad without you. I love you so much."

"Oh my God, Balunn … I've missed you more than you know. I love you too," Savannah said as her arms tightened around his neck and her mouth smothered his beautiful full lips.

He nuzzled her ear gently and whispered, "I think you're ready now for me to make love with you."

"I think you're right."

The End

About the Author

Kay Chapman has worked as a registered nurse and midwife in a wide variety of settings throughout her forty-five-year career: teaching hospitals, private hospitals, military hospitals, charitable organisations, community clinics, home birthing, and remote areas. She retired in 2015.

This book was first written, in its most rudimentary form, in July 2003, and only in retirement has it come to light. It was inspired by the many wonderful people the author encountered throughout her career.

Kay is married and has three birth children and two stepchildren, joined by their partners and subsequently many grandchildren. She is grateful to have lived such a varied life and thankful to be able to present this story to you. Enjoy!

Printed in the United States
By Bookmasters